Advance Praise

7 Doors of the Firemaker Is a modern allegory that delivers thought-provoking messages about real-world issues, both internal and external, that all of us face today in some form or other.

Through the metaphors of the Seven Doors and the Firemaker herself, the author presents an identifiable way of looking at life and life events that can help us deal with life challenges like loss, recovery, and questioning that can lead to discovery, personal triumph and fulfillment.

This is a book that will resonate with anyone interested in attaining a more peaceful, understanding, and uplifting life. It's a book you will carry with you in your physical journeys and reread every few years so that its messages are not forgotten.

– *Carolyn Hamilton, Author of* Hard Amazon Rain *and other books*

Marina Walker Rose brings all of her genius as author, teacher, gifted therapist, celebrated artist and playful feminine to this multilayered tale of a young woman as she moves through a labyrinth of seven doors into an expansive world of self-discovery. As if a story woven with color, movement, symbol, and whimsy was not enough, Ms. Rose gives us more, and we are compelled to follow. Her visceral, masterfully structured companion notebook becomes our personal passageway, opening us to our own labyrinth of discovery; its brilliant visual design and content creating the very pathway to being our most authentic selves. I eagerly await the workshops and women's circles that will undoubtedly be born from these timely jewels.

– Robin King, Labyrinth facilitator, spiritual counselor and channel.

If you're ready for transformation and soul evolution, pick up *The Seven Doors of The Firemaker* and its companion notebook. This novel is told as a fable, and its notebook takes the reader through each of the seven doors to transformation.

Being a very human reader, I wanted to know more about what had happened to the protagonist Helen to make her the way she was, what made her begin her search. Yet after I realized that I am Helen, and you are Helen, the author's intent became clear to me. It doesn't matter what trauma happened to us, it's how we move into our inner world and thus, into the future, that matters.

The brilliant accompanying notebook lets the reader travel through the doors just like Helen does. That's the step at which change occurs for you. The workbook is there by your side with questions and guidance. It can be used individually, but it's also a great book for coaches to use with their clients and for workshop use.

"Deep down you already know, but it never hurts to be reminded, that magic is normal," the author says in her introduction to the notebook.

Go find a little magic, or a lot. It's up to you.

– *Kathryn Brown Ramsperger is a master intuitive coach and trainer and owner of Ground One Coaching as well as the author of the award-winning novel* The Shores of Our Souls.

If you're looking for an adventure that allows you to forget the day to day grind you've come to know, Seven Doors of the Firemaker, is it! A colorful journey into a secret garden that holds insights into one's subconscious you didn't even know existed.

From first page to last, the author's writing style will captivate and engage you.

– *Kathleen Gage, Best Selling Author of* PowerUp for Profits

Marina Walker Rose's magical way of storytelling has created the perfect soul-searcher's guide to the world we are living in now. Her novel and the companion notebook offer women and all who have known hurt, heartbreak and loss an empowering new way to live and move forward.

– *Elena Ibarra Wellness Consultant, Holistic Health Practitioner*

In every individual, in every moment, there exists the potential to become something greater, to evolve, to truly recover and know they are whole. These are the words of The Firemaker and the story of my journey through the Seven Doors with Helen and Marina Walker Rose. With Marina's guidance and gentle care, and my willingness to take the journey, I have smashed my Pearls, survived Shrapnel, broken down my City of Stability walls, uncovered my Sunstone, and set sail on my Downstream Dream towards my City of Joy. The journey is open to all who seek to shine their unique light in the world. Join us!

– *Lorraine Hall, Writer, Non-Profit Controller*

Beautifully written with heart, Helen's journey is one of determination and hope as she bravely enters the magical Land Behind the Doors. This enchanted story is rich with metaphor, steeped in insight, and changing worlds. A Beekeeper, a talking frog and a waitress named Sugar, not to mention the Firemaker, are only some of the many memorable characters we meet on Helen's search for a little piece of the Sun. In Marina Walker

Rose's *Seven Doors of the Firemaker* she gives voice and expression to complicated struggles and feelings, bringing them honor, relevance, and compassion. This is a book you will keep, and you will want to read again and again.

– Diadre Quinn, Human and Organizational Leader

Seven Doors of The Firemaker

A PERSONAL AND PLANETARY ADVENTURE

Second Edition

Marina Walker Rose

THOMAS NOBLE
BOOKS

This work was originally published in 2005 by OakStar Press. It's been revised and updated for this new edition.

Thomas Noble Books
427 North Tatnall Drive, #90946
Wilmington, DE 19801
ISBN: 978-1-945586-18-7

Editing by Gwen Hoffnagle
Original Art by Marina Walker Rose
Cover Design by Sarah Barrie of Cyanotype.ca
Internal Layout Design by Balaji Selvadurai

For little Helen who walked alone.

You have been found and brought home.

Dear Reader,

Since *Seven Doors of The Firemaker* was first published, much has changed in the world at large. You already know about the big world stuff. How could you not?

As the world watches, there is a wave of people speaking truth to heal themselves and safeguard others from the pain they've endured.

Their voices matter.

Those who are sharing their stories find themselves on a journey they hadn't planned, in need of action in a way they never sought or imagined.

Whatever has happened to you, whatever wars you've survived, you've walked into a New Room that's big enough and bright enough to allow for a whole *new story*. The seal to the Old Room has been broken. Undone. The one who became the many walked out, looked up, and claimed, *"No more!"*

Seven Doors of The Firemaker tells the story of a young woman named Helen Brower who goes on a great life-changing adventure in a place called the Land Behind the Doors. Like that wave of people speaking their stories to heal and end human-caused suffering, in this second edition of the book Helen speaks about a part of her story that she didn't share the first time around. But it was always there, tucked into her heart, until the time came when she was ready to tell us more.

You will discover why Helen left home; why she's always sad and tired; why nothing she tried (and she tried everything) changed anything. Knowing enough to know that she had to leave, her journey began when she realized that what she needed most could not be found where she'd already been.

In the Land Behind the Doors, may you find something special and true to light the way as you undertake *your own* adventure through the Seven Doors; because you *will* go through them. Everybody has to, sooner or later, because things irresistibly realign themselves with time and experience, and none of us are immune to that truth. I call that reality *The Law of the Ice Vanishing and the Erosion of Soil*, or *L.I.V.E.S.* for short. It's an unavoidable natural law, and I live under it just as you do. No one and not a single thing can escape it.

It's understood by simply recognizing that glaciers melt and topsoil washes away or is blown somewhere else by the wind. The timeless beauty of *L.I.V.E.S.* is that there's always something worthwhile, even astonishing lying beneath the visible that's just aching to be revealed. You know it. You can feel it.

Since I first wrote *Seven Doors of the Firemaker*, my *whole self* has discovered important new truths and subtleties buried beneath the surface of my life experience from before my birth until now. Revealed by contemplation, hindsight, and the Grace of the Universe under natural law, my right timing arrived with the sonic shattering of two simple words of truth claimed around the world during a year of awakening and enlightenment that changed everything: *Me too.*

Hope springs forth from what is lost. Above all, the second edition of *Seven Doors of the Firemaker* is a story of hope. I wrote it to help you with *your* journey through the doors, whatever your life experience, age, or identity; and because it is the nature of the world to evolve, and a story is a living thing that keeps on showing you more if you're patient and know how to listen.

Who am I? Well, today I would describe myself as a paint-slinging mystic artist cosmic adventurer guide who also happens to be a little bit of a cheerleader. While some parts of Helen's story are autobiographical, it's not about me — its intent is and always has been to empower *you* to melt the ice and wash away the surface soil of your being, so you can get to the priceless stuff that lies buried beneath. What is hidden there is wonderful beyond belief. What is hidden there is YOU.

I offer you this evolution of the story of Helen, a rudderless, frazzled, lonely-but-bravehearted young woman whose search for her place in the world takes her through the Seven Doors of The Firemaker on a magical and magnificent quest for knowledge, fulfillment, and yes, love.

If the stars align — and I fully expect they will — what happens for her will happen for you, too. When it does, you will be astounded by the fact that you were standing on top of the *real* you, your *whole self you*, all the time, all your life.

When you come to the end of the book, I invite you to come with Helen and me in *The Firemaker Companion Notebook* to begin your own journey through the Seven Doors. With the right map and tools, and a good measure of cosmic magic along the way, you'll have what you need to navigate your way from Old Rooms into New Rooms, one door at a time — strong, tall, and lit up from within.

Marina Walker Rose, Spring 2018
Seven Doors of The Firemaker: A Personal and Planetary Adventure
The Firemaker Companion Notebook: A Very Human Cosmic Explorer's Guide

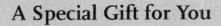

A Special Gift for You

Marina Walker Rose has created two guided
meditations especially for her readers!

Please visit: MarinaWalkerRose.com/readergift
to download your meditations.

Table of Contents

Prologue

(Please don't skip this part!)

One way to find the missing piece you're looking for and I know you're looking for it – is to get off the bus that Virgie drives. Then, a day later, you ride your old yellow Huffy bike down the hill toward the garden and into, well, you'll see.

If you decide to go this route, the garden's in the back, behind Peri's house, which sits on the banks of the the Little Dreamy. Watch out for the cats.

For me, it wasn't all that far to Peri's House and the rest. Well... yes it was. In truth, I guess I was both near *and* far.

I wouldn't have said this before my journey in the land Behind the Doors, but now I know that often those words, *near and far*, as just abstractions, fuzzy doodles in the head without any firm mooring in reality. Tug on them just a little, and they shift.

More times than not, *near* sits facing the back of far on the Ring of Life like a couple of people riding tandem on a bicycle.

Far is just us expecting that what we desire could only exist somewhere a long way off. *Far* is just us bending our sight all the way around the Ring of Life and right back to *near*, where what we wanted had been sitting right next to us all the time.

What's *that* mean? It means that sometimes if we'd simply *turn around* we'd find ourselves already standing within arm's reach of our destination.

It's shocking to realize that we can be living in separate realities simultaneously, each reality at loggerheads with the other.

We might be outwardly steeling ourselves for some epic journey that stretches out far ahead – a quest to finally reach that elusive goal of *inner peace and power*. But at the same time we may secretly believe at the center of our being that there is absolutely no way for us to ever get there at all.

Often, that is when Life unexpectedly intervenes, keeping us on track in spite of our split realities. The next thing we know, we turn around and bang! There it is! Right next to us, hiding in plain sight where it had been all along.

It's a tricky place, the Ring of Life, lots of smoke and mirrors. Lots of illusions, misdirection, and shifting sand beneath the feet. It can make it look as if *nothing* but an epic journey will get us there. And sometimes that's true. But not always.

Don't get me wrong, an epic journey can be compelling and infinitely interesting and I'm about to share *my* epic journey with you. Obviously I believe it's important or I wouldn't be doing this.

The trouble with an epic journey, though, is that it's always so darned much work. But I happen to think that once you hear my story, you just might be empowered to save yourself some very interesting *far*, turn around, and jump right into the *near* that holds what you're looking for.

That could mean skipping a lot of the lost time you would have to invest if you went it alone, not to mention the dramas.

Here's the thing: I know that no matter *who you are*, the First Door is always *near*, waiting for you to enter. Regardless of appearances, this has always been true. Just as it's true that the help that comes along with going through that door is waiting for you, too.

Even if it *feels* as if you're all messed up, even if you've been feeling that way for year and years, you can enter and help will be there to guide you. It might be anybody or anything.

It might be a waitress, a beekeeper, or a frog, but somebody or something will be there to help guide you if you will make that first leap of faith.

I'm living proof. You can go in that First Door with blurry vision, a broken heart and no idea what you're doing. And you can come back out of the Last Door absolutely whole with light in your eyes and fire in your heart.

When that happens, things you've never known will be known. Creative possibilities you've never dared hope for will burst out like spring flowers. And those invisible but nasty traps you keep stepping into that hurt you so badly will stand out like one of those giant red, light-up noses that circus clowns wear.

Even more important, there's a very good chance you'll discover that being intuitive and aware does not require you to walk around with a long, serious face. And being courageous doesn't mean you have to lose your joy or develop a hide as thick as leather. But you'll see what I mean by all of that later.

Now let me tell you about my adventure...

CHAPTER 1

Misery or Miracles

Remember Alice? In Wonderland, I mean. Right. *That* one. Well, if you ask Alice, or me for that matter, we'd both have to say it's amazing how fast you can get sucked down a rabbit hole and into the adventure of a lifetime.

That's exactly what happened to both of us, except *my* rabbit hole turned out to be a seat on a bus right behind Virgie Washington, city bus driver. I didn't know it at the time, but when I got off at my stop, less than ten minutes after meeting her, the rabbit hole had me. And when my journey was over, my life was changed forever.

It began like this...

Following some strategic problems with gravity and the weather requiring a little help from Virgie, I finally got on the bus after waiting twenty minutes at a stop just off the freeway. You know the kind, just a sign with a picture of a bus and a bench with no shelter over it, zero help when it's raining buckets, which it was.

By the time Virgie pulled up, the rain had worked its magic and the bottom of my overstuffed brown paper bag had turned to oatmeal. She eased the bus to a stop and opened the door.

In keeping with several of the major laws of physics, my little stash of groceries, tuna sandwich and Diet Coke, all met the sidewalk at precisely the same time, then headed off in as many directions as they could manage to head off into.

Up to that point, my whole life had been a lot like that. Rain coming down, bottom falling out. You understand. My life was a tapestry of wars and flowers, and yawns.

Unfortunately, there had been many more wars than flowers, and the yawns, of varying lengths and intensities, dotted my landscape like wildly proliferating weeds.

Actually, right at that moment, my life resembled an extended yawn, but that didn't mean there wasn't pain, too. There was, and lots of it.

But the main thing to know about all of that right now is that if you grow up in a family that hits instead of hugs, screams instead of talks, and makes wounds instead of mending hurts, you end up with a kind of primal ache that never goes away.

It becomes systemic. It's as if there's this disgruntled organ called *pain* that doesn't work right – or maybe it works too well. And it's sitting there right inside you, along with your spleen, stomach, lungs, and all the rest of it.

In my case, I got out from under all of that on a Sunday afternoon a few weeks after I turned sixteen. Slipping away unnoticed as my parents screamed at each other about something – probably wrapped around me – I had done, or not done, or should have done better. It had happened hundreds, if not thousands of times before, but in that pivotal moment I knew it was time for me to leave, and I left.

It was such a nonevent in a way. No drama. Just a little tip of my imaginary hat to two people who didn't notice I had been leaving inch by inch for a long time in my heart anyway. It was strangely simple. I left a note, walked out the front door and never went back.

> **Dear Mom and Dad,**
> **I'm leaving. Sorry...**
> **Go ahead and rent my room.**
> **– Helen**

It wasn't very eloquent, I admit, and it was at best cynical and way light on gratitude or details. I wouldn't do it that way today. After all, they'd clothed, fed and housed me since day one of my life. But they hadn't loved me in a way that I could grasp onto. To be honest, I'm really not sure they loved me at all, but if they did, they sure did a good job keeping it hidden from me.

But back then, I was just a lost little kid, a teenager; I didn't know one-tenth of one percent of what I know now. I didn't know my true nature, or why I felt so bad any more than I knew what to do about it. And my concept of a *bigger picture* was sketchy at best.

Anyway, I don't recommend what I did to anybody, especially kids. All I can say to young people facing a similar challenge is, as they say on TV when some guy is about to try to jump the Grand Canyon on a motorcycle, "Don't try this at home."

It can be brutal out there on your own. I didn't have a compass. I didn't have a map. I was just that nuts guy on the motorcycle at the edge of the Grand Canyon of Life with only my raw emotions for fuel. Looking back, there were surely other paths I could have chosen.

But I was extremely fortunate. I survived it and things fell into place when I most desperately needed them to. Actually, that's why I'm telling you all of this – how by a so-called chance meeting things stopped falling apart and instead started falling into place.

And ultimately I'd have to say that leaving home probably saved my emotional life. I *know* it saved my sanity. It took me out of a certain kind of harm's way. But what it didn't do was stop the pain. That came right along with me.

Something else was going to have to fix the pain problem and so far, at least up to the moment I met Virgie, whatever that something was remained as elusive as a winning lottery ticket.

Romance didn't do it. Work didn't do it. Food didn't do it. Alcohol and pills didn't do it. Buying stuff didn't do it. Pretending everything was all right didn't do it.

Those were all the big and little wars I'd fought and survived during the ten years since I permanently walked out of that house and away from my family, and the only thing I knew for sure was—they didn't do it.

"I'm sorry I can't help you with all that mess there, honey," Virgie said, "but if I get out of the bus and somebody sees me, they'll have my hide back at the bus barn."

As she spoke, the rain decided to let up and turn itself into a light mist, thank God, making things a little more bearable as I gathered up my stuff.

"I've got this plastic bag here if you want to round all your things up in it," Virgie said, leaning down and handing me the bag. "Take your time. Nobody on here but me today and I'm about seven minutes ahead of schedule."

"I appreciate it, thank you." I even managed a little smile as I knelt there glancing up at Virgie between scoops of stuff, my hair limp as spaghetti.

"Story of my life," I said, almost more to myself than to her. "The bottom is always falling out of something around me."

Virgie nodded and smiled while I herded the debris into a pile. "Everything's always falling apart huh? I hear ya, darlin'. I know all about it. You got all your stuff there, now?"

I picked up the last of it, a squashed plum and soggy notebook, looked around and decided that was all.

"Yeah, I think that's it."

"What's your stop?"

"Thorne. Thorne Circle."

"Thorne. Got it."

Virgie shoved a plump hand into a big blue backpack beside her seat and yanked out a small hand towel and another plastic shopping bag, then dove back in for something else. Patting the space on the seat behind her, she held out the towel, the plastic bag and a banana.

"Here you go. Come sit here behind Old Virgie. We'll get you dry, fed and where you're going. You can use this other bag for a rain hat if it's coming down when you get off. What's your name?"

I plopped down on the seat, slowly dried my face and hands then began eating the banana.

"Helen. Helen Brower."

Virgie peeled a banana for herself then eased the bus onto the freeway.

"That's a pretty name. Helen," she said, with a nod of her head. "It's old fashioned. I like that."

I smiled, thanked her, sighed, looked out the window, and took a big bite of the banana.

Virgie looked at me in the rear view mirror. "Plastic sure is a miracle, isn't it?"

I considered that for a second, realizing I'd never thought of plastic as anything but a blight on the ecosystem. But when you really stop to think about it, plastic gives us miracles all the time. We just have to figure out a way to keep the magic and get past the harm. It has its downsides, but there are a lot of miraculous things you can do with plastic. Like keep your stuff dry in the rain.

Just then a thought dropped into my head, as if someone were piping it in from a remote sound booth: What other miracles are you ignoring in your life, Helen?

It startled me because – at the exact same moment – the rain stopped and there was a break in the clouds. Sunlight shot through and the day brightened beautifully.

That's a miracle right there, I thought. But before long, I was deep into my problems again.

Virgie and I rode for about five or six minutes in silence.

"Wanna' talk about it, honey?"

"Pardon?"

"Do you want to talk about it?"

"It?"

"About you looking flat worn out and me imagining it has nothing to do with this rain and your bag falling apart."

I wobbled my head faintly from side to side. "It could be so much worse. I mean, if this is as bad as it gets..."

"Excuse me for interruptin', honey, but sounds to me like you're quotin' not talkin.' Talk to me."

I had to laugh. If Virgie hadn't stopped me, I'd have rambled on another ten minutes, never getting to it.

"The truth is I am worn out. I need a job. I don't have a single lead and, well, you get it."

"Sounds like nothin's workin' out, right. Is that it?"

I nodded. "I don't know what to do, Virgie."

"What would help?"

"I wish I knew. A job would be a huge breakthrough. At least that would put out the financial fires, if not the rest of them."

"Maybe what through the open door into th you need is MORE fire, not less."

"Sorry?"

Virgie smiled, "Oh, nothing honey. You said Thorne's your stop, right? It's up next."

She began to slow the bus and ease it toward the stop.

"Thanks for keeping track. I'd have completely missed it."

I got up, quickly gathered my things, and walked up next to Virgie and waited for the bus to stop.

"Thanks for everything, Virgie, especially the banana. It hit the spot."

Virgie gave me a broad grin, followed by a serious look, the kind that goes right into the very center of you. Then she smiled again.

"A banana sure is a miracle, isn't it? Even better than plastic. I'm sorry we didn't get to talk longer, Helen, but here, take this."

She reached into her breast pocket and pulled out a little notepad, clicked her ballpoint pen and wrote something down.

"It's gonna be okay, honey. You go home and dry out. Have a good sleep and call this nice lady in the morning. She's got what you're looking for."

I took the paper and glanced down but didn't read it.

"Looking for? I don't know what you mean, Virgie. Oh, you mean work? Really!?"

Virgie chuckled. "It'll be work all right, various kinds, too, but good work. You can count on that. Just call her. She's good people."

She reached for the lever and opened the door.

"You call that number tomorrow and go see this woman, hear? She'll fix you right up."

Virgie patted me on the arm as I placed my hand on the rail and headed off the bus.

As I stepped down, I looked at the paper and saw the name

"Peri" and a phone number. I wasn't at all sure what she was sending me into, but my instincts told me that Virgie was all right, so wherever she was sending me would be all right, too.

"Thank you, Virgie," I said.

At the bottom of the steps I stopped and turned to face her. And that's when the rabbit hole snatched me for sure.

It lasted only a split second, but there was no mistaking what I saw – a flash of sunlight from a gold band on the middle finger of Virgie's right hand, and a burst of scarlet above her head, like one of those rare-blooming cactus flowers that come out of nowhere after a heavy rain.

But this wasn't the desert and Virgie wasn't a cactus, so I blinked and shook my head hard. Maybe the banana hadn't been enough. Must be low blood sugar. I thought that must have been it because suddenly, there was Virgie the bus driver smiling down at me, same as before. And before I could say anything, she spoke again.

"Don't worry, Helen," tapping her heart and then her head. "Pretty soon, you'll understand."

Then she closed the door, waved and pulled off down the street.

CHAPTER 2

Peri

The next morning after breakfast I made the call. The woman at the other end of Virgie's mysterious phone number was a little quirky, but pleasant and lively enough.

It was some kind of gardening work. Though still winter, in this part of the country the weather is so typically mild, gardening goes on pretty much year round. I love plants and I'd done a bit of gardening before. So I figured, what the heck, maybe she'd hire me. With her address scribbled on a scrap of paper, off I went.

The way to her house was uphill, a hard ride on a bicycle. Long since faded from her original buttercup glory, that old bike had carried me through more than a few adventures. Other than on foot and the bus, sweet old Dolly was how I got around.

It was nearly three o'clock and I was struggling to peddle Dolly up the hill. I needed this job to tide me over until I sorted things out and could find something more substantial. On paper it wasn't a bad plan. But in reality I'd been trying to "sort things out" my entire life. Bad outcomes always seemed to follow me, my decisions ending in disappointment and regret. With a big gulp of air, I pulled the zipper of my blue windbreaker all the way up and summoned one final burst of energy to make it up the last hill.

After a few wrong turns I found the address. It was a modest house, white with navy trim. Locking Dolly safely to a weathered YIELD sign on the corner, I walked up to the porch, patting my hair into some kind of reasonable arrangement and tapped the brass knocker gently against the dark blue front door.

A breeze had come up, stirring the faraway tones of a wind chime. I waited a few seconds and tried again. This time, the door swung open. Scuffling noises and a loud thud were quickly followed by three cats shooting past me and out the door.

"Hello? Is anybody here?" I asked, hesitating for a moment before cautiously pushing the blue door open the rest of the way...

It smelled like oranges and earth, a comforting combination that eased the rowdy thumping in my chest as I hovered in the doorway, listening for footsteps and a friendly voice.

The fiddle-shaped leaves of a potted tree almost as tall as the ceiling had grown over a pair of slipper-tucked chairs. Each a brighter shade of yellow, their dimpled contours lit up the cozy entry like sunflowers on a cloudy day and I wanted more than anything to sit in one of them and rest awhile.

I didn't, of course. But I did take a step, just one through the open door into the entryway where the walls were covered with colorful paintings of boldly shifting shapes that felt good to look at as I stood and gazed past the yellow chairs, baskets of mud shoes and newspapers, and into the great room.

A flagstone and tile-finished fireplace burned bright and steady next to a worn looking green sofa with turned legs and patterned pillows that mirrored the long-faded carpet – a velvet blur or emerald, garnet, and sky. Save for a well placed woolen throw and the pillows, the sofa was empty.

Suddenly something brushed my shoulder. I turned and saw a peach-faced lovebird flit to safety on a nearby perch. Too fat and slow to do more than trot after her, a tabby cat settled nearby on the arm of the sofa.

Chattering and mocking, the bird scolded the cat, whose tail twitched back and forth in time to the lovebird's rant. Head cocked, feathers fluffed, the tiny bully took full advantage of her safe perch, stirring the other birds to join in, which they did. There were many and I also spied several canaries, another lovebird, some finches, and varieties I didn't recognize.

Just as things really began to get out of hand, a woman's voice rang out from the hallway, "That's enough, Lil! That goes for you, too, Henry! You've got to stop taunting each other! You know better than that!"

Waving an old broom, she burst into the room. Lil squawked once or twice and settled into preening her feathers. That's when the woman spotted me.

"Holy Moly, who the...?" She let her question trail off but kept the broom cocked at the ready over her shoulder.

I quickly backed up. "Whoa! Hang on! Hang on! My name is Helen. We spoke on the phone? I called about the gardening job?"

"Goodness sakes!" The old woman quickly lowered her weapon and chuckled. "Of course! Helen! Forgive me, my dear. Afraid I got my overalls in a twist again over those two. It's the second time today!"

"I'm sorry I walked in but I heard the commotion and thought..."

"Oh, shoot, forget about walking in, honey. Door was probably open anyway, usually is. That lock's been broken forever. Been meaning to fix it, but meaning to isn't the same as doing it, is it?"

She walked over to the door and closed it with some kind of special maneuver. "See, if you don't lift up on it when you close it, it doesn't shut right. And then all the heat gets out and I spend the next hour kvetching about it to the animals."

"They must get sick of it, but that's what I charge 'em in rent – listening to me whether they want to or not. They're stuck with the arrangement, poor babies. But it's not like they're gonna band together and go rent an apartment, is it?" She laughed at her own joke then said, "Sorry I startled you."

Pulling a small yellow handkerchief from somewhere in her sleeve, she mopped her forehead and laughed again. "Name's Persephone, but you can call me Peri. Everybody does."

"Hope it's not too warm in here for you," she said, taking my hand. "I can't stand the cold."

"Had way too much of it when I was a kid in Toronto, and now I've got a zero tolerance policy. I like to crank up the fire pit out on the patio, she said, chuckling. Keep 'it blazing almost half the year."

"That's an interesting name you have there, Persephone. Don't think I've ever known anybody with that name before."

"I wouldn't think so. It's unusual, that's for sure. My mother was a poet, and a bit of a philosopher, too."

"She loved magic and ancient tales, and that's where the name Persephone came from – from a Greek myth. But not one child in a hundred at my school could pronounce it, much less spell it, so I nicknamed myself Peri and that solved that."

"I'm afraid I'm not too up on my mythology."

"Oh, don't worry about it. Nobody is these days. If the story ever needs telling, I'll be happy to, but that's not important right now."

"Anyway, it's nice to meet you, Helen," Peri said, smiling and putting down her broom to shake my hand. I couldn't help but notice how the wide gold band on her right middle finger glinted, even in the fading afternoon light of winter.

"How about having tea with me and we'll chat. It's kind of chilly today. A good day for a nice cup of tea."

"I'd like that," I said, following Peri down the hallway to the kitchen. "Again, I'm sorry about barging in unannounced."

"Don't give it another thought, my dear. I've been expecting you. I meant to greet you at the door, but I got busy with my orchids, and then that blasted pair of troublemakers. You know how it is when you're doing something you love."

"The orchids, I mean, not chasing the animals. You lose track of time, but enough about that. Let's have a cup of tea, and then we'll take a look at my poor old garden out back."

Peri had one of those smiles that transform a face. It pillowed her cheeks from ear to ear, lifting her wide brown eyes into a pair of lopsided ovals of well-traced lines.

As she talked, her strong, knotted hands kept time to every word.

"Did you come a long way?" she asked, buttoning her sweater up to her chin.

"Not so far," I said, adjusting my windbreaker. "I rode my bicycle here – I must look a terrible mess."

Peri laughed. It was a lively, gentle laugh, kind and happy. "No, kiddo, you look fine. I was just wondering if you live nearby, that's all."

"Sorry. I get a little nervous with new people and tend to talk too much and say the wrong thing."

"I used to have a little of that in me, too, when I was your age. One of the best things about getting old is that it gets you over the minutia. Like having tangerine hair when you're 79. But you know what, who cares?"

Peri was obviously enjoying her life, something I wished I knew how to do.

"A sweet with your tea, dear?"

I helped myself to a cookie, thanked Peri and looked out the window, waiting for my tea to cool.

"Drink up, dear," she said a few moments later. "It'll take away the chill and then we'll have had tea together, and we won't be new people to each other anymore."

I nodded, had a sip, and then answered the question from before. "You asked about where I live? It's about three miles from here on the cul-de-sac over on the other side of the hill. I just moved there a few months ago."

"Cul-de-sac, oh, that would be Thorne," Peri said, nodding. "Well then, it wouldn't be too much of a hike for you to come to work."

"No, not much," I told her, a little hesitantly. "Not once I get used to it."

"Every time I look out this window," Peri said with a sigh, "I remember why I love this part of the country so much."

"That one never goes completely barren," she said, pointing out the window toward a bonfire of a bougainvillea bush. "Big Bella gets sun all year long, and unless it's an unusually cold winter, just keeps flowering and flowering."

For the next half-hour, Peri and I sat and drank tea and talked about gardening. She explained that she owned this property and the house we were sitting in. Her land also included a large, walled garden she'd cultivated from bare ground many years before. Peri lived off the grid. Along with her many trees and solar-paneled windmill in the back, she kept chickens and harvested rainwater, avocados, citrus and stone fruits.

The more Peri talked, the more I wanted the job. And as much as I wanted it was as much as I worried. I worried that something would go wrong. I worried that if I got it I might not be able to keep up. I worried that if I said yes to her I might not like the job and want to leave.

But even in the state of mind I was in back then, I knew these worries were nothing more than little lies I told myself because I was scared. Scared of what, I'm not even sure. Disappointment maybe? Hurt? Failure? Getting close to someone?

In the end though, all those lame ideas and fears didn't matter because the truth is, I needed to do something more than I needed to be afraid.

And besides, this quirky old woman with her orchids and her fire pit and bird-and-cat wars made me feel good in a way I hadn't felt in a long time. With a bit of luck, maybe she would hire me after all. And maybe I would like the job, even be good at it.

Peri began to explain the situation. "I live alone, contentedly these days, raising flowers and fruit trees and, as you saw, fooling around with my precious animals."

"But I stopped tending the garden years ago, but – well that's a story I may tell you later. Anyway, I've got a bit of arthritis in my hands now, so even though I'm ready to bring the garden back to life, I need another pair of hands, Helen."

As I listened, my eyes swept the pleasantly cluttered room, coming to rest on a large purple orchid, a *phalenopsis*, Peri would tell me later. Set out in a ceramic container in front of the bougainvillea-framed picture window, it bloomed in the midday sun that also bathed me in its light. It was a moment I could almost have eaten.

"If you're finished with your tea, Helen, why don't you and I take a look at my garden? But I have to forewarn you, it's quite a mess."

We put on our jackets and walked out the back door of the kitchen and around the outside of the house to a thick wooden gate behind some large bushes and cypress trees.

A big brass lock fastened the hasp. Peri took a key from her pocket, unlocked the gate, and pushed the door inward. Creaking on its rusty hinges, it opened into a tangle that was more thorn than green. Still, it was glorious and held a quiet so full and calm, I instantly made it my own.

I knew I belonged in that garden. I can't tell you how I knew, but I knew. The pull of it on my heart was insistent and real.

As the door swung open, I could have sworn I heard my name, spoken as softly as a feather on the wind.

An instant later, a cardinal flashed past, diving from the highest tree, crying softly as he skimmed the perimeter of the garden. In that moment, something awoke inside of me, and all I wanted was to be in the garden and stay forever.

I turned to Peri, "Even if your garden *is* a bit disheveled, I love it here."

"Me, too. You can awaken into your *whole self* in the silence and quiet growth of a place like this."

When Peri spoke those words I felt a strange natural power expanding in my chest like the endless blue of a summer sky. Something big was beginning, and I sensed it.

"Come on, let's go further in," Peri said, touching me lightly on the shoulder. "My great grandnieces are coming to stay with me this summer. Before they get here, I want to see the garden back in order."

She smiled her sweet smile and pushed up the sleeves of her sweater. "As I told you, these old fingers don't work so well anymore, but with your help, we can put it back together. I'm not quite done with gardening yet."

We walked the length of the old garden, bordered by three walls made of stone, one in the front and two on the sides.

There was no back wall. The garden gradually sloped down the hill to a small river running by at the bottom. Just at the point where the river began to turn from view, it curved into an inlet where a little blue sailboat was docked, rocking gently back and forth, up and down with the current.

Peri pointed to the water. "That river down there is the *Little Dreamy*. Pretty thing, isn't it? Full of fish and turtles, and there are hundreds of ducks on it every summer."

"A river's the simplest and yet the most complex thing in the world all at the same time. It's all of creation flowing by Life just going where it's going."

Peri gestured in a sweeping motion toward the overgrowth. "But as for this mess, you can see, there's a lot of work to be done. Think you want to take it on?"

I looked around the garden and down at the Little Dreamy. Without turning back to face her, I nodded and said without hesitation, "I do."

Peri nodded back and grinned. For some reason, I'm not quite sure why, Peri's words, *awaken into your whole self*, hit me again, and I knew instinctively that I was in for more than just a gardening job.

When that thought had made it about half way across my mind, Peri laughed softly, as if she'd heard every word. I turned around to face her.

Then it happened again. Another rabbit hole moment.

For just a split second, as it had been in those last few moments with Virgie when I was getting off the bus, there was a flash of scarlet above her head, and from her golden ring, a burst of brilliant sunlight. But just as I finished turning, Peri was standing there, the same as before.

"Everything okay, Helen?"

I didn't know what to say so I deflected with, "Oh, I'm just a little tired from the ride up the hill. But I'm all right."

Peri smiled and nodded, and I had the strangest feeling that she knew exactly what I'd just seen.

"Okay, then we'll start tomorrow," she said. "I'm glad you're here, Helen."

"Me too, Peri. You don't know me, but thanks for giving me this chance. "

"Oh, I think I have a pretty good line on who you are, Helen, and I like what I see. Wouldn't hire you if I weren't certain that it's a fit for both of us. You run along home now dear and we'll get started early tomorrow. Eight o'clock sound all right?"

"You bet. I'll be here, Peri. See you then."

CHAPTER 3

The Garden

I came back to Peri's the next day, and the day after that and many more days after that, working here and there in the garden, often deep into the most forlorn and tangled parts.

It was hard at first, almost too hard because I wasn't in the best of shape back then, but that had more to do with me than with the job. In those days, just about everything wore me out.

But it got easier after a while and in some strange way I didn't fully understand, being there was incredibly comforting. It was as if I was one of those disheveled, neglected plants myself, becoming healthier and stronger as the gardening progressed.

Peri gave me lots of room, which also accounts, in part, for how comfortable I felt. She didn't bark orders at me or ask a bunch of intrusive questions.

Mostly, I was left to choose the tasks I wanted to accomplish each day. I would spend time with her in the greenhouse, or the job I liked most of all, pressing further and further into the garden's most tangled overgrowth.

That time by myself, knowing Peri was nearby if I needed her, was like a balm for all that pain inside of me.

When we did work together or rest in the late afternoon in front of her fireplace, Peri's presence, at times as wild as the garden, at times as steady as the Little Dreamy, blanketed me in safety and a feeling that was as close to joy as I had come in a long time.

I didn't know then how it was that Peri understood what I needed, but she did. She knew it was going to take me time to get the hang of things, just as she also knew I was there for more than a job and that I was in serious need of healing.

When I was tired or a little blue, she would encourage me to grab one of her cats and go sit under a certain especially large Live Oak tree she'd named "Aunt Betty."

With my head resting against Aunt Betty's massive trunk and a cat purring in my lap, I could almost feel the current of life, flowing like the Little Dreamy, back and forth between the river, the tree, the cat, and me.

As I cleared and planted in the garden, my mind often drifted with the flow of the days into memories of my difficult and lonely childhood.

I was the youngest of three and the only girl in a family that – as I have explained – was as disheveled and thorny as Peri's garden without the promise of anything beautiful emerging from it as I knew the garden eventually would. In spite of that, I could also remember a time when I felt different about life, a time when I felt lit from within.

Back then, when I was a little girl, life seemed bursting with possibilities and I woke every morning ready to greet them. But as I grew older, that inner light dimmed and clouded over. All that was left was a kind of hazy malaise that seemed to blur what had once been joyful into nothing more than the memory of a past too painful and far away to help me feel anything, let alone dream of what could be.

I wasn't planning on telling you more than just a little about my childhood before. But by now, you have a pretty good idea of the state I was in when I came to Peri's house, so it might be helpful to know how I got that way. Sadly, it's not all that uncommon a situation.

The events on the unhappy planet of my childhood chipped away at something vital in the center of me. Instead of color and song and joy, I was filled with sadness and illness and giving up.

Every hurt, every neglect, had left wounds in places invisible to the naked eye. Years of hiding in plain sight, years of not being seen by my family for who I really was, taught me how to live a small, abbreviated existence.

Oh sure, for a long time I did my best to resist, to fight for my truth and the right to *be*. But in the end the battle overwhelmed me and darkness had seeped in through the cracks in my being.

Still, I can remember a time before all that happened, a time when I was all questions and shining eyes.

I must have been about five when I asked my mother the most important question of my little life thus far. And I'll admit she gets credit for a good try on this, too. Better than most of her tries, even if her astrophysics *were* a little flawed.

Obviously it's impossible to remember it exactly, but our conversation went something like this:

"How did the world get here, momma?"

"The world? You mean how did the planet – how did Earth come to be? "

"Yes, how did the world get born?"

She hesitated, then said, "Well, a long, long time ago, when the sun was a lot bigger than it is now, a big explosion happened. Nobody really knows why."

"But it shook everything in the sky and knocked off a chunk of the sun and that broke into a thousand pieces. Those pieces went spinning into space, and one big fat piece started spinning around and cooling down until it became the Earth."

"And what about the rest of the pieces? Where did they go?"

"They went all over the place and made some other planets. I think. They made our galaxy or something."

"Did any pieces fall down on the ground *after* our piece started being the world?"

She let out an exasperated sigh. "Lord, Helen, I don't know! This is why I never do this with you! One question answered leads to fifty million more." She shook her head. "If you're so darned curious, go out and see if you can find yourself a piece of the sun!"

By this time the big needle on my mother's Brief-Interpersonal-Moments-With-My-Beloved-Daughter meter was in the red zone. "Be a good girl and bring me something cold to drink, Helen. Momma's busy."

I was used to that last part, and besides, I pretty much had what I wanted from her anyway. So I fetched her iced tea and out

I went to spend the rest of the day wandering around in a little haze trying to sort through the information I'd gleaned.

Because my mother had said so, it must at least be *possible* that there was a tiny piece of the sun lying around somewhere. And if it was out there just lying around somewhere, well, somewhere could be *anywhere*, so it was also possible I could find it.

Dipping further into my innocent, little-girl logic, if a person found something as magical as a small piece of the sun, then it made sense that something absolutely wonderful was bound to happen, right?

I spent the whole afternoon searching our tree-lined street, which was the entire universe to me, thinking I would find something, some evidence that what my mother said was true. I was sure of it. There might be a dark burn mark on a lawn, or a little crater behind the grocery store. *Something.*

But nothing happened that day, or the next, or the next and before I realized it, I'd spent the entire summer in pursuit of a little piece of the sun.

I've been on the fence about sharing this part with you. But now that we're here, I've decided that it's important to speak plainly about things that are hard to speak plainly about. Even if the thing you need to speak plainly is another person. Even if you love them.

Mom liked things tidy, pretty, and most of all, sweet. But no amount of sugar will make a foul tasting thing wholesome any more than it does a foul acting person. When I told my mother what Uncle did to me, she punished me for lying. And then she made me go back. Who would believe the word of an eight-year old girl already forgetting that she's whole over a city council member and retired principal, beloved by all? Sometimes the truth just isn't enough to make a person believe what they *don't want to know.*

Every Tuesday afternoon when I was six I went to his house after school. He lived two blocks from us, in a one-story ranch house with rust-colored drapes that always seemed to be drawn. It was an arrangement that worked out well for everyone, except me.

I didn't remember those Tuesdays for many years. But after my journey behind the doors, I remembered it all, the shame and the ugliness – and the thing that was *none of that.* I called her the Red Fairy. In the dark hours of the morning something wondrous came to comfort me. Her ruby-gold light filled my bedroom with the kind of glowing warmth that makes your whole body just-let-go. She took my hand in hers and off we went to beautiful, far away places that smelled like cinnamon and oranges and roses. I spent many hours with my crayons and pencils and little box of watercolors drawing pictures and writing stories about the Red Fairy and me.

CHAPTER 4

The Search

My childish drawings and relentless search for my little piece of the sun provided endless fodder for family ridicule, especially since I didn't find it. Well, at least not back then.

"Clumsy Helen's hunt for a piece of the sun" was just one of many crueler and humiliating games my family never tired of playing.

Before it was all over, I'd stuffed a hundred such longings deep inside and begun to pretend they didn't matter. That was where the trouble began, pretending what I wanted didn't matter. Over the course of my life, I became an expert at that.

My mother's neglect and father's rage shut away my memories of the Red Fairy who came bringing comfort and peace and the glowing red warmth that once shone so brightly in my heart.

Looking back now with adult eyes though, I can happily tell you that despite the pain of those years and my eventual master-level capacity to camouflage my feelings, something vital and worthwhile survived the process.

Something always whispered to me that my life could be different, and that the sum of my broken parts could eventually manifest into something extraordinary.

I suspected that I would eventually find a way somehow to take those parts and form my life into a beautiful galaxy too, just as those broken pieces of the sun had done.

Longing for a greater understanding about what life meant and how it all worked stayed with me and I continued in my own way to search for what I suspected was out there, even though I couldn't see it.

When school started that year, I secretly kept looking for my piece of the sun. Maybe, I thought, just maybe I would find the meaning of things by looking where it wasn't so bright. But as with so many people, the years passed and the ultimate understanding I so desperately sought didn't come.

After a while, I almost forgot about that primal day and a time when I truly believed in something. Yet even forgetting what had started my search didn't completely banish the vague-but-persistent suspicion that I would find the answer somewhere, someday.

In the process I learned to look closely at the little things because sometimes it's the seemingly insignificant things that reveal the underlying truths or universal laws, laws that could open the doors to discovery and fulfillment.

I kept thinking that if I paid attention, and kept noticing the great and the small, if I just kept expecting to find something important in all of it, there was at least a chance that one day I'd find what I'd lost of myself. And then I would be whole again just as I had been briefly when I was living the happy little-girl version of me.

That seemed like a reasonable idea, but getting there wasn't so easily done. By the time I was ten, instead of waking up ready to greet the day, confusion and anxiety would fill my being with an endless stream of questions before I even had time to get out of bed.

Why am I the way I am? Why do I feel all scattered and sad? What am I doing here, anyway? But there were no answers.

Slowly, but persistently, something akin to the exact opposite of my little piece of the sun came into being; it was as if a small, cold asteroid had formed in the center of my chest. As time passed, it grew into a kind of painful dead zone inside me that never left. I now know that it would take a very specific lesson from the most unusual of sources to show me exactly what I must do to be rid of it once and for all.

Years later, as a teenager, a pivotal moment came that would eventually lead to that source.

I'm not quite sure anymore what happened that day. It was some argument or upset around the house – I don't exactly remember. I just know I was exhausted in every way a person can be exhausted. When I went to bed that night, I knew I was heading into a deep sleep.

But when I arrived at that nether place between sleep and waking, a voice spoke out to me. It seemed to come from somewhere inside my room but at the same time from inside my head:

"I am The Firemaker.
Seek me and you will find me.
Find me and you will be whole."

Needless to say, I was frightened and sat up so quickly I banged my head on the bedpost and nearly fell on the floor. I mean it's not as if a disembodied voice talks to you every day, is it?

Later, when I'd calmed down and realized what had happened, my fears turned to downright elation. At least something was finally responding to my pain.

Of course, my next realization was that I had absolutely no idea what the mysterious statement meant, much less where I was supposed to start looking for whatever this Firemaker was.

I lay awake for several hours hoping the voice would come back and offer more clues, but there was nothing. After thinking it over for a while, I realized that it didn't matter. I knew that I would leave home the next day, regardless. It was time, and knowing that was what mattered.

And I also knew that I'd find The Firemaker if it took the rest of my life, whatever it required. Having made those decisions, to leave home and search for The Firemaker, relaxed me to the core and I quickly fell asleep.

As I slept I dreamt of a place so incredibly warm and alive, a place so much a part of me that wherever I went in the dream, it transformed into what I knew was my true home.

I never saw her in the dream, but I knew instinctively that The Firemaker was there with me, close by but unseen.

I knew that somehow, some way, I would find her and learn what I really needed to know to be whole and have a full and wonderful life.

CHAPTER 5

The Little Dreamy

At the end of each workday in the garden, long after the light had gone, Peri and I would sit together by the fire, taking in the evening and the cool, moist air that blew in off the Little Dreamy.

Although Peri disliked the cold, she always kept a window open so the breeze could come in and the cats could call her through the screen to let them in.

Bundled in a blanket on the green sofa, I reveled in the music of the river and the feeling of soft fresh air in my lungs. And in her whispered kiss, I heard Evening's promise that I would soften, too.

Spring was approaching. She would come first with paper whites and hyacinths. The crocuses had already pierced the hard winter ground. Soon their tiny, hopeful heads would send brilliant explosions of saffron and yellow bursting into the garden. After that, the green-budded fruit trees and first strawberries would not be far behind, and then the violets would come.

Out there, just beyond the limits of my vision, the Little Dreamy ran downstream to the ocean. Just knowing that, just embracing that inevitable reunion of fresh water with its mother, the Sea, delivered a calm I'd longed for but never known.

The sound of the river told me I was in the right place in my search for The Firemaker. The Little Dreamy was making its way home – and so could I.

CHAPTER 6

Discovered Treasure

As I said earlier, just like Alice in her trip through Wonderland, I was well into my journey before I fully knew it.

In some ways, it started the day my mother told me about the piece of the sun and continued when the voice spoke to me, when I left home, when I met Virgie, and when I went to work for Peri.

But the day my search for The Firemaker really moved into high gear was the day I was standing in Peri's garden steadily cutting back the tangled mass of bushes growing along the southern wall.

Suddenly the clippers clanked differently than before. Parting the leaves, I slowly opened an area to the light and found, much to my surprise, a small stone alcove. Much wider at the bottom than at the top, the recess sloped upward to a gently curving point, creating a tiny altar in the garden wall.

I continued to cut away the tangled growth until I uncovered a small square ceramic tile about four by four inches at the base of the alcove.

When I brushed the dirt away I could see a child's version of some kind of wheel had been painted on the tile, then glazed and fired.

"Peri?"

"Uh-huh?"

"Can you come here a second? I think I've found something interesting."

Peri took off her gloves, leaned her spade up against a wall and walked over to me. She gently stroked the small tile as though it were a living thing and smiled broadly.

"You found one of the little altars! I told you this garden's full of secrets."

"You mean there are others?"

"Oh, yes. Had them built in when the walls were being done. There are seven, all covered up like this one I'm afraid."

"Where'd they come from, Peri?"

"Well, my sister, Sophie, has a daughter, Rosie; Althea and I did them with her when she was little."

We used to have a small kiln back here. Made ceramics, little pinch pots and these tiles and such. I'd like to do something along those lines when *their* girls come this summer."

"I like it. It's very sweet."

I'm glad you like it. They're each special in different ways and it's going to be so nice to have them out in the light again." Peri patted my arm and went back over to her spade.

There was something beyond delightful about having discovered the little altar. I guess it confirmed for me that the garden was not only starting to take shape, but revealing her treasures, too. And so was I.

I felt good about what I'd accomplished, but even better about how Peri was becoming a friend and mentor. As I said, she gave me plenty of room and she didn't hover or want more than we'd agreed upon.

That method worked wonders with me and I found myself settling in, maybe for the first time in my life. There was a pride I took in it all, a warm, clean feeling that in large part because of my work, Peri and her family would fully enjoy the garden again.

Over the next few weeks, I uncovered five more altars in the side garden walls, each with a different tile, just as Peri had said.

Peri had chosen to leave the overgrowth inside the front entrance wall for last, and it was there that I found the seventh altar. But when I found that final one, the tile was missing.

I called out to let her know I'd uncovered the last altar and to ask if she knew where it was.

"Look, Peri. This altar doesn't have a tile. Do you remember what happened to it?"

A shadow seemed to fall on her face as she let out a deep sigh. "There's a reason why I put off clearing up the front entrance wall for last and why this altar was never finished. Come with me to the potting shed. I think I still have – well, just come along and I'll explain."

We walked out of the garden and back toward the house and a small potting shed where all the materials and gardening tools were stored.

I'd been in there many times but never had a reason to open the small cabinet on the back wall. Peri opened it and inside were two ceramic tiles, one with a drawing of some kind of flower and the other with an image of a candle. She reached in, took them out, and handed them to me.

"Here you go, honey. Take these home with you tonight and you decide which one to put up in the last altar. I really don't have a preference."

"You see, what I haven't told you is that I had a twin sister, Althea. We called her Ali for short. Ali passed away a long time ago, here in the garden, actually, before we had time to cement in the last tile."

"Oh, Peri! I'm so sorry. I had no idea."

"No, of course not, dear. I never told you because it's still painful. Some things you just never quite get over no matter what. We were as close and connected as pearls on a necklace, so losing her was pretty hard."

"As you can imagine, the garden took a long time to create. We loved working on it and playing with our nieces down by the Little Dreamy so we were in no hurry. We worked on it for years."

"Ali and I were out here one sunny fall day, just the two of us. The girls had made two tiles before they went home at summer's end and left them in the kiln to be fired."

"Actually, that was creating a bit of a dilemma for us. There was only one altar left to decorate, but Rosie had made two tiles so, well, we weren't sure exactly what we were going to do. As it turned out, that decision never had to be made – until now."

"Anyway, we were doing all the stuff you and I do, planting, watering, pruning, all of that. I was down at the back on the open side of the garden, and Ali was sitting against the front wall beneath that last altar."

"I called to her to bring down some potting soil but she didn't answer. It was such a lazy day; I just thought she'd gone to sleep, so I didn't pay much attention at first. But then I got the strangest feeling."

"I walked up and called her name and nudged her shoulder but she didn't stir. I knew right then that she was dead, but I tried to revive her anyway. Nothing worked. The doctors said that her heart just stopped, that it happens sometimes."

"No warning, and thank God, no pain. She sat down for a little snooze and never woke up again. Never had a single symptom. So you see, it was a lot more than arthritis that stopped my gardening."

"After Ali's funeral, I locked the garden gate and went on an extended trip. When I got back home I just couldn't come out here again, not until the day before you arrived."

"But this experience is something I want to give to my grandnieces, like Ali and I had done for their mother, Rosie, when she was a child. So all this sprucing up the garden, reliving the memories of Ali and Rosie making the tiles, and letting the garden nurture someone like you, well, I didn't want to leave any of that untouched before I die."

"And it turned out that you were the perfect person to accompany me through this rebirth of the garden. I knew it the moment I laid eyes on you. Old Virgie has pretty good instincts. She was right to send you to me."

"I'm so so sorry for your loss, Peri. Now it all makes sense. There's more to that Virgie than meets the eye, isn't there?"

"Oh, yes! Lots more. She's a real treasure, and one of my dearest friends."

"I'm a strong woman, Helen, if I do say so myself, but losing Ali nearly killed me. Just when I needed a friend most, I literally bumped into Virgie at a swap meet and we just hit it off. She'd lost someone special, too."

"After the swap meet, we had coffee and she told me how she came to understand her pain was just life putting her on a different path, an inner journey I could go on as well, if I wanted to take it. And take it I did. Now, thanks to Virgie, that journey inside is something I absolutely cherish. It's made me whole despite losing Ali."

"Still, some things just have their own life cycle, their own time frame, and nothing you do can speed it up. I miss Ali terribly because we were such wonderful friends. But I've made my peace with her passing and I imagine her off doing something lovely on the other side. I'll catch up with her soon enough."

"For years though, my work was inside *me*, not in the garden, and I was sure that I would know when it was time to open it up and go back to work. And I was right. Lots of people answered my ad just as you did. But when you called, I knew you were the one. That same day I came out and entered the garden again for the first time in—forever."

"Sure enough, it's a pleasure to be working in it again, and especially to share it with you."

"Oh, Peri, thank you so much for telling me! The garden means even more to me now, and I was already in love with it, and you, too. You're the dearest, sweetest friend. Thank you for sharing all this with me."

"My pleasure, Helen. I feel the same about you. Now enough about the past and my troubles. You put these tiles in your backpack and scoot on home. Sun's starting down and I don't want you out on Dolly tonight. Looks like it might be clouding up to rain."

CHAPTER 7

The Accident

Peri was right, it had rained during the night, so the roads were still wet the next morning when I rode my bicycle toward her house.

I was coming down the last part of the steep hill, gliding into the abrupt turn at the bottom when a little girl dashed out of nowhere into the street after a ball.

Slamming the brakes, I managed to miss her but turned too sharply to keep my balance. All I remember is Dolly shooting out from under me. I went flying and landed hard, skidding onto my side until I finally crashed, headfirst, into the concrete curb.

As I lay on the ground with things going dimmer and dimmer, my thoughts went to Peri, the garden, and the little altars with their lovely tiles.

Then everything faded away into nothing.

CHAPTER 8

The Land Behind The Doors

"Wake up, Helen" a voice whispered so gently I thought I was dreaming. I moved my body cautiously, but there was no pain or blood. Everything seemed fine, until I looked around. I was in Peri's garden, that much I knew, yet it was so different. The garden had shed all signs of winter, and the air, now warm and bright, was scented with sweet perfume.

"Where am I?" I said out loud.

"The Garden," said the voice.

It had returned! After so many years the voice had come back. But how? How could this place, this sudden summer, *be*? I tried to collect myself but inside I was all scrambled up.

"How did I get here? "

"You're awakening," said the voice. "The Garden is where you need to be, and I am here to help."

"*Who* are you??" I called out. "Where are you?"

"I am The Firemaker. You have been seeking me for a long while, have you not?"

"Firemaker?? You're here!?"

"I'm here. Turn toward the tree you call Aunt Betty."

I turned toward the center of the garden, toward that familiar tree. A woman was standing beneath Betty's green branches in a hooded robe the color of sunrise. It glistened and flowed over her body like a living thing, covering all but her chin and mouth, which curved into a tender smile.

I audibly gasped. As if to affirm what I was feeling, she spoke my name and lifted her right hand. On the middle finger of her right hand she wore a thick band of gold. A flash of sunlight shot from it to me. I could only stare and keep breathing.

"How–how–long have you been standing there?" I finally managed stammer.

"I have always been beside you, Helen."

"Always? ...But I've never seen you!"

"Your eyes were closed to me. Your ears heard my call but once. Even so, I've been here with you, always."

Still I was not comforted and a chill ran up my spine.

"But...why can I see you now?" A horrible feeling began to sweep over me and I panicked.

"I'm dead, aren't I? I died in the accident, didn't I? I finally pushed Dolly once too often, and now I've gone and killed myself! Oh, god, I'm such an idiot!"

The Firemaker laughed softly. "No, Helen, you're not dead. Or an idiot. Far from it. You're just ready, that's all."

"Not dead?"

"No. You're very much alive."

I could feel the muscles in my neck and back start to relax. "If I'm not dead, then what *is* this place?"

"This is your natural state of being, though not a state of consciousness you would call normal.*"

"But that's another conversation for another time. What you need to know now is that you have found me, and you are in a state of readiness, just a few steps from the Land Behind the Doors."

"The Land Behind the Doors? A state of readiness?"

Now I was really starting to get nervous. In the years I'd spent imagining this moment, I'd never thought past finding The Firemaker. It had never occurred to me that I'd have to *do* something once I found her.

"If you decide to take the journey that awaits, in due course you'll understand that, and much, much more. But these things can't be explained simply. You will have to work to understand."

I nodded my head, my mind spinning with questions and confusion and everything was happening so fast. This was big and I was going to need a kind of courage and stamina I didn't have.

But I couldn't walk away, so I paused, and began again.

"The last thing I remember I was riding Dolly, my bike, and then a little girl ran into the street after her ball. I tried to avoid her but I crashed, I think. And, well, suddenly I'm here and it's summer."

"It's a lot to take in, Firemaker. I'm going to need a few minutes to get my bearings, if that's all right."

"Of course, Helen. Take all the time you need."

That calmed me and I suddenly remembered there was something I had to know.

"If it's okay, I have to ask. Your name, or title, or whatever it is, *The Firemaker*, what does it mean?"

"If you do the work, you will know in due time. That's all that I can tell you because you wouldn't understand now. Preparation is required."

"Preparation? Preparation for what?"

"For living your life differently."

"You've been unhappy with things as they are, yes?"

I nodded.

"And you've long sought a new way of being?"

I nodded again.

"This journey, if you complete it, will mean that you never have to go back to the way things were. It won't even be possible to go back."

"Are you sure, Firemaker? All I seem to do is climb halfway up a mountain, and then something happens and I slide back down, over and over. But what if I can't do what you're asking? What *are* you asking of me, anyway?"

"See the doors, Helen, the ones along The Garden wall?"

I looked at what had once been small stone altars with children's tiles embedded in them. Now they had become full-sized doors.

"What happened to the little altars?"

"Changed. This is the place for change. Those are special doors and if you pass through the experiences that wait on the other side they will change your life completely. Some of it will be thrilling, some of it unsettling, but all of it will be worthwhile."

"If you make it through seven doors, you'll undergo a metamorphosis as radical and dramatic as that of chrysalis to butterfly. And you'll discover something important about humanity and your relationship with the planet."

I thought for a moment. Yes, this was *big*. "I hope you don't take this the wrong way, Firemaker," I said, a little nervously. "But is stopping allowed? My track record isn't the best and I might need to take a break or two along the way. It might be smart to know the rules up front, if that's okay with you."

"Of course" she said, her voice warm and encouraging. "In these tasks, you decide whether you want to continue. You can stop at any point. But, if you choose to go forward, even if you cannot see me, know that I will never be far away, as it has always been between us."

"Okay. That makes me feel better."

Here I was, faced with what would likely be the first of many decisions to come. I walked over to Aunt Betty and sat down, my back against her great trunk. She was strong and steady, and as I leaned into her I thought about what I'd experienced in my life and how lost I'd felt so much of the time. Other than Peri and my gardening job, there was nothing much to go back to.

Don't get me wrong. Peri and the lovely garden were wonderful, *way* more than wonderful. But I needed more.

Something enormously important was missing, even if I didn't know what it was. I got up and faced The Firemaker. Well, *faced* might not be the proper word because, as I was to learn, I would not see her face for a long time.

"You've made your decision?"

It was unlike me to decide quickly back then, but for some reason I didn't hesitate.

"Yes," I told her, "I have. I want to do this."

I wanted my life to change. As I saw it, the world was a colossal disaster, and what good *did* exist, well, that always seemed to be for other people, not me.

"Firemaker," I said, drawing a little circle in the grass with my foot. "I'm not a very confident sort of person, but you probably already know that. It's just that I would hate to fall short."

"Be easy with yourself, Helen. It took great effort to even reach this starting place. Be pleased that you found your way here at all, and please don't be too concerned with whether you'll finish or do well. I've spoken of what *is* possible, but whatever you get done will be absolutely transformational and wonderfully beneficial, I assure you."

"There's time to rest before we begin. There's even time for you to change your mind. Just be still within yourself and leave your worries with Aunt Betty. She'll comfort and calm you."

"See the green hammock? Spend time there. When you're ready, walk The Garden's path and try to really look, *really see*. Let The Garden show you *Life*. You'll know if this is meant to be, and exactly when it's time to begin."

So, I stayed.

And while somehow time wasn't really time in The Garden, I remained there for what seemed like weeks, curled up in the green hammock. I meandered down the path, following the trails of beetles and flights of dragonflies. The Firemaker was always nearby but said little.

I thought my time in Peri's garden had rested me from the weariness that was always with me. But here in The Garden with The Firemaker, I could see there was more to my fatigue than I knew. It ran deep. Soul deep.

Even if nothing more had happened beyond spending that special time in The Garden, I believe just being there would have transformed me because everywhere, absolutely *everywhere*, was LIFE. And for the first time, I was truly seeing it.

There were many varieties of trees growing in The Garden, not just Live Oak, but Liquid Amber, Willow, Avocado and Fruit Sisters, Peach and Plum, their sturdy branches bent low with juicy goodness, aching to be picked.

Nearby, Poppy pushed up through The Garden's rich soil. Skimming the green, Quick Sparrow swooped and said hello to Buttercup and Rose. Hummingbird joined them, kissing the nectar from Jasmine and Lily. Green serpent vines, heavy with ripe cantaloupe beads wound through Morning Glory, crossing fields of Marigold, Starling and Junegrass.

Everything in The Garden answered summer's call, from the plants and the animals to the lush, cool, clover-covered slope of the hill and the pure, crystalline water of the Little Dreamy below.

Then, the moment of certainty came. Like a newborn foal that knows in an instant she can run, I knew that I was ready. I turned and glanced over my right shoulder. As usual, The Firemaker was there. I took a deep breath and whispered, "Now."

The Firemaker nodded and motioned toward the First Door.

CHAPTER 9

The First Door

The tile on the First Door was decorated with a painting of a wheel, not the kind on your car, but the lottery kind, the spin-and-take-your-chances kind.

I looked at the door and then at The Firemaker, even though I knew I wouldn't see her face. But I was used to that by now. In all the time I'd spent wandering The Garden, I'd never seen more than her smile peeking out from beneath her hood.

Glancing at the door again I asked, "What do I do now?"

"Simply push it open and walk through. Not too fast and not too far. There's something on the other side you'll want to talk over with me."

"Okay, here goes." I pushed the door open and slowly stepped through it, The Firemaker following close behind. It didn't take long to see what I was up against. I was standing on a narrow ledge atop a steep cliff, at least several thousand feet high. I nearly fainted.

I quickly turned to run back through the door, but The Firemaker had already closed it behind us. Heart pounding, I looked toward her, mouth dry as a wad of cotton, and pointed to the wide, empty sky.

"This is a mistake! It has to be! What the heck am I supposed to do up here!?"

"Well, first of all, why not try and get all you can out of the experience? Why not take a minute and enjoy the view?" She touched my arm softly and I instantly felt more centered, if not all that brave.

Summoning my courage, I took a few slow, deep breaths to calm my racing pulse, and then gently stepped closer to the edge near The Firemaker. The view was spectacular!

Sunrise opened the sky and the valley awakened into morning. Far below I could see a long line of people no larger than ants gathered at what looked like a country fair. I felt clean and light and enjoyed the breathtaking view. But, still, I was so afraid my knees actually shook, not a very good way to start an adventure.

Suddenly, a terrible realization hit me. I knew what was next, or at least I thought so. "Wait a minute!! Hold on! You don't want me to climb down this cliff, do you?"

"Of course not, Helen."

"Whew!" I laughed nervously. "That's a relief."

The Firemaker nodded. "Yes. I imagine it is. What you have to do is jump."

"Jump. Jump? JUMP??? I don't think so! I'm willing to try new experiences, within reason of course, but I'm not jumping off this cliff!"

"I understand, Helen," The Firemaker said quietly, almost tenderly. "If not for the fear, you would like to try, wouldn't you?"

I peeked over the edge. "It's a little hard to imagine not having any fear."

"Yet you have managed to imagine this without fear. Do you remember pretending to do this as a child? Leaping out, soaring like a hawk down into a pretty valley like this one? You've pretended that, haven't you?"

"Yes. I did. But this is real and that was just make believe."

"There's less difference between the two than you might think, but I understand. Tell me, what do you think you would need to make it possible to take the leap?"

"Well, good luck, for one thing— a lot more of it than I'm used to having."

The Firemaker opened the palm of her right hand, "Very well, take this pouch. It contains what you ask for. Here, let me hang it around your neck."

She stepped around behind me and draped the strings of the pouch over my head. "There. All the luck you'll ever need. Now, are you ready to jump?"

"Wait, wait, WAIT!" I yelled, nearly hysterical. "I don't care how much luck you've got inside that little pouch — it can't be enough! I need something else, maybe a rope or something? Maybe a parachute?!"

As soon as I'd spoken the word "parachute," I felt the weight of a pack on my back and straps fastened to my body.

"How'd you do that?"

"You might want to consider it a method of advanced goal setting. If you manage to pass through seven doors, you'll discover a Cosmic Law that explains how this works, but that's a long way from this moment. Right now getting your gear squared away is more important."

The Firemaker adjusted the parachute's harness a bit then pointed to the cliff. "There you go, Helen. Now you can jump."

I held my hand up and stepped back as far from the edge as I could. "Hold on a sec. I don't know how to parachute. Isn't it sort of mathematically precise? I mean, don't you have to calculate wind factors and drop-weight velocity and stuff?"

"Well, it's actually quite simple. You stand right there, on that big rock, and jump off."

"Then what?"

"Well, because of the Law of Gravity, you will immediately begin falling quite rapidly toward the ground."

"Hmmm. And then?"

"And then?"

"And then how do I keep from getting squashed like a bug on a windshield if something goes wrong, like a rogue wind blowing me all haywire? I could get killed!"

"You pull the cord, Helen. Here, let me place it in your hand. When you've had enough free fall, just yank it. The longer you wait, the more exciting it is. That's all there is to it."

"But if it doesn't open, or I do it wrong, it won't be pretty!"

The Firemaker laughed softly. "Just a short time ago you thought you were already dead. If I hadn't told you differently, you'd have thought *this* was the afterlife, correct?"

"Yes, I guess so."

"Then just pretend I was mistaken and that you're already dead. And besides," The Firemaker said, pointing to my neck, "you have your lucky pouch. I don't see how you can lose."

I reached for the pouch, gripping it tightly in my hand. "Thank you, Firemaker. I hope whatever else is in here, it's got new batteries."

The Firemaker chuckled softly. "Try to relax, Helen. The pouch and parachute will work just fine. Simply follow the instructions I've given you and everything will come out perfectly, I assure you. Enjoy the ride."

And then gently, "I will see you again, Helen. Look for me at the Little Bridge."

CHAPTER 10

Spinning

I turned my attention to the edge for a split second and when I turned back to ask The Firemaker where I would find this Little Bridge, she was gone. My heart sank. I looked over my shoulder at the terrifying drop. It didn't look any better no matter what angle I took.

"Ohhhhhh, this is not good!!"

So there I was, completely terrified, alone, thousands of feet up with no escape, and no way off the ledge but to jump.

I decided that yanking on the doorpull was a good idea, but when I did it was locked. "Great!" I shouted, then spun around and timidly looked down the cliff face once more. "One foot out of the gate and I'm already in trouble."

"FIREMAKER! Oh, FIREMAKER! I'd like to discuss this a little further!"

But there was only the sound of my own voice echoing against the mountain.

At my feet was an overhang, jutting out barely wide enough for me to stand on over a sheer cliff with no trails and no way to climb down. After several more tries at the door and many looks down for some other way out, I finally surrendered to the situation.

Clutching the pouch in one hand and the ripcord in the other, I stepped out onto the ledge, took a deep breath, closed my eyes and leapt.

I got over the thrill of free fall very quickly, barely off the cliff when I yanked the cord. The parachute opened with a loud *whop!* As it billowed and opened fully, I knew that I was going to be all right.

Just as The Firemaker had said it would be, I soon found the feeling wonderfully exhilarating, so much so that I laughed and kicked my feet as I drifted through the marmalade sky.

Several minutes later, I softly landed on an enormous feather bed in the middle of a large open field. The parachute collapsed, covering me in nylon, or whatever they make those things out of these days, and I lay quietly until everything stopped spinning.

"That was wonderful," I said to myself as I unbuckled the harness. The air had a slight chill to it, and I rubbed my shoulders to warm up, laughing as I rolled off the bed and onto my feet.

Far across the field people were lined up by the dozens at the gates of what I could now clearly see was an amusement park.

I began the long walk across the field. It was an easy stroll, flat and even with no rocks or gullies. Reaching the other side, I spoke to the first person I met, a sturdy soldier with a red beret. "What's going on? Why such a big crowd?"

"The Big Deal Wheel," she said.

"The what?"

"We've all come to try our hands at spinning the Big Deal Wheel. I'm telling you, everybody does it, absolutely everybody."

In the distance, I could see the giant Big Deal Wheel whirling round and round. It was a formidable sight, but the eager and hopeful faces of the people standing in line didn't appear the least bit apprehensive.

"Here," the soldier said, "jump in front of me. Nobody'll mind."

I thanked her, but as I stepped in line the lady behind us burst out, "Hey! Just a minute, toots! Who do you think you are? Wait your turn like everybody else!"

Toots. That didn't sound like a good start.

The soldier turned around and snarled something nasty at the woman who made a rude gesture and growled back, "Go bang your ankles!" They went at it for a full minute until I finally stepped out of line.

I said to the soldier, "Hey, look, it's not worth it. Thanks anyway."

I told the other lady I was sorry and headed for the end of the line. That didn't seem to help much because the two continued flinging insults at each other, but at least I wasn't in the middle.

When I finally reached the end of the line, I joined the others as they waited, moving ever closer to the Big Deal Wheel. It towered above the stage, shiny and fierce atop an immense platform lashed down by cables and crudely set pins.

People filed in from the right, up a short but steep flight of stairs where they took their spin, then left, walking down another flight of stairs at the opposite of the stage. A pair of guards stood watch, one beside each staircase.

Vendors had set up nearby, hawking pizza and pretzels. There must have been an area for livestock, too, because the air reeked of hay and dung. It was loud and crazy and not the least bit fun, though I know lots of people enjoy amusement parks. At best, I appreciate the *idea* of them, but the reality, well... I think it's more hype than fulfillment. When I find myself at one, I try to stand back and observe what's going on.

That's how I noticed some of the people looked about as happy as a person can look, twirling like children as they exited the stage. But many didn't seem nearly so cheerful. Disappointment screamed from their mouths and haunted eyes. And I felt sad and eager to be done with whatever this door was about.

Spanning the length of the stage, a loud green banner proclaimed the rules of the game.

THE BIG DEAL WHEEL

What Goes Around Comes Around.

And underneath that, just barely visible to the naked eye:

Caution! While this equipment is made of the finest materials, the manufacturer makes no warranty, implied or written concerning its use. Spin at your own risk. Dreams, Wishes & Surprises Industries, Inc. Magic, Illinois

As I waited and continued to watch, scores of people took their turns, and the line slowly inched forward. By now the morning air had become sticky and insufferably hot. But the line kept growing, never seeming to diminish. The energy of the crowd was unstoppable, giving up bursts of applause at random moments. But something didn't make sense. The prizes weren't what anyone would call life changing. And you couldn't count on them going to the person who'd just spun. It was little more than controlled mayhem.

A lot of what came from The Bid Deal Wheel was cheap as prizes go; magazine subscriptions, fuzzy key chains and such. But some of the stuff was pretty sweet, like an island vacation for two, new summer dress, a cuddly puppy.

It was nice to watch people have these happy moments, but they were few and short lived, and—I hate to tell you—most of what I saw was not very nice at all. Flat tires, parking tickets, cell phone overcharges. You know, life's annoying little nuisances. It gets worse. For the truly unfortunate ones, well, let's just say they got stuck with things likely needing a lifetime to recover from or forget.

"I didn't want that!" or "Yippee! I finally got it!" or "Why is this happening to me?" they yelled as a half dozen purple prom dresses and as many hula-hoops landed on their heads. A storm of dried-up Christmas trees nearly suffocated a group right in front of the stage and a well-dressed woman in a blue business suit got a pink plastic tiara and five-year term in prison for embezzlement.

Bad hair days, splashy weddings, husbands who came home and wives who ran away. These and all kinds of large and small triumphs and tragedies came into the lives of those who spun the Big Deal Wheel. I could sense something connected these people to what they received, but I had to watch for a long time before I figured out what was really going on. Those who spun were not the random winners or chance victims they'd first appeared. It's hard to explain how I knew. I just knew.

The more I watched, the more I noticed how many, both lucky and unlucky, got back in line for another spin. It was a funny thing, though, because I could never predict how they'd handle it. Some who faired well behaved as if they expected nothing less, while less fortunate repeat spinners acted as if they deserved whatever bum goods The Big Deal Wheel spat out at them.

With few exceptions, those who got something truly wonderful rushed back in line for another spin of The Wheel and a chance at something even better.

Watching their faces it seemed that the good feelings that came with these moments of success were short lived. People grumbled about what they'd gained and lost, never quite satisfied with what they had, even if it were something you or I would have at the top of our bucket list.

For a few bliss-filled moments, I figure, they had a shot at, well, *everything*. The anticipation of something new, something better than they already possessed, was fabulous. Better than fabulous, it was life itself and they couldn't get enough. Who could? As with many things this intense, the yummy, expansive feeling that came from spinning couldn't be sustained. Once it began to lessen, the need for it set in again.

By now I'd been at the amusement park most of the day and seen a lot of disturbing stuff. There were people of different ages, some of them well appointed folks, while others had been clearly beaten up by life. Yet there was something they all had in common. I could see it in the clench of their jaws and the droop of their shoulders. It was as if spinning had become a joyless task they wanted to stop, but couldn't.

Lucky or not, spinning was a ride to the *Big Yes! - a* roller coaster on the high arc of *possibility*. At least I suspect that's how it felt to them during those final moments before the wheel stopped.

You'd think after getting burned a time or two, folks would move on. But the veterans, they seemed to think that as long as they stayed in the game, they still had a chance at something more, something greater for themselves, and their families, too.

In some ways I really couldn't blame them. When you've been doing something for a long time, it's hard to stop. Even harder to imagine there might be somewhere else where you could find the good feelings and fulfillment you've been seeking.

With the heat and the drain of so many deep insights, I was feeling a bit unsteady on my feet when suddenly I found myself at the head of the line. Mind you, a lot of what I'm telling you I've figured out only through hindsight. At the time I was mostly just disgusted and confused about why I didn't leave.

"Surely," I reasoned, "The Firemaker must have guided me here for a purpose, even if I don't know what it is."

But the feeling that I should leave this place and press on with my journey kept building inside of me until I wasn't sure what to do. Something powerful told me there was an alternative to this that was better and that I should just walk away. RIGHT NOW.

But I didn't. I just stood there in one of my all-too-familiar clouds of indecision. As I got into full scale faltering mode, I suddenly had a sense of déjà vu. I'd been here before! I'd stood before the Big Deal Wheel!

My revelation would have to wait. It was *my* turn to spin!

At last, I told myself, I too would have a chance to get something good, something that might make me feel more alive inside. That's why I was here, right? Feeling more alive was what this journey was all about, right?

A spin at the Big Deal Wheel might solve part or even all my problems. Heck, it might give me what I needed because I was no different from the people in the park. They all needed something, and so did I. I just didn't know what.

The heat of the moment made it impossible to think clearly, and besides, the crowd was nudging me on, shouting, "Hurry Up! Hurry Up!"

I lifted my arm to wipe the sweat from my forehead and wondered vaguely, "Why am I doing this?"

But the crowd pressed forward, screaming in unison, "Spin the Wheel! Spin the Wheel! Spin the Wheel!"

"Everyone's waiting, what else can I do?" I said under my breath and began to climb the stairs. I must've been moving too slowly to suit the people behind me because the crowd started to get angry. I caught a glimpse of the soldier who'd been so kind to me before. "Hurry up, dammit!" she shouted.

Over the uproar and the pounding of my heart I couldn't hear what else the soldier was saying, but I probably wouldn't have liked it anyway. So, I grabbed a peg on the Wheel, tightened my body to gather the maximum force, and spun.

The Big Deal Wheel crackled and buzzed and whirred as it turned. A huge picnic basket full of kittens flew out and knocked the soldier down.

Then a brief thunderstorm of expired credit cards pelted several people in the crowd, and a tiny blue monkey leapt from shoulder to shoulder, yanking off men's toupees and peeing on women's shoes. It was ugly.

Finally, as the Wheel slowly stopped spinning, a small drawer popped open at the bottom. *Ka-ching*!

I reached in for my prize and pulled out the only thing there, a soggy fortune cookie.

I looked around, stunned. "This is it? A stupid fortune cookie? All this waiting and leaping off a cliff and all I get is a soggy fortune cookie?"

Now the crowd was screaming wildly. "Open it! Open it!" They yelled. So I broke the cookie open.

The crowd went silent and I heard the soldier shout, "What does it say?" as I read to myself:

GET OFF THE STAGE!

I couldn't believe it, but there it was. I grimaced, shook my head, and held the little strip of paper up to show them. "Um, well – it says, 'Get off the stage,' actually."

Immediately the crowd broke out in a chant like this was some kind of college football rally.

"Get the hell...off-the-stage! Off the hell...stage! Get the hell... off the stage!"

From the looks on their faces it was obvious they weren't just repeating what I'd read, either. They wanted me to get the hell off the stage. *Now.*

I smiled sheepishly, stuffed the strip of paper into my shirt pocket, stuck out my tongue and hurled the crumbled fortune cookie at the crowd. I'm not proud of that, or of what I screamed.

"Phooey! You people make me sick!"

All I can say in my defense is that it was a truly horrible experience. Stumbling across the stage I ran down the steps in a daze. Now what? I looked up at the faraway cliff where this adventure started, then around the valley. At last I spotted the giant bed and set out toward it across the field.

When I reached it several minutes later, I collapsed on top and drew the parachute up around me. Just before giving myself over to sleep, I reached into my pocket, held the strip of paper to the sky and read it again just to make sure I wasn't mistaken. I wasn't.

I wadded up the paper, flicked it into the air and muttered to no one: "Big Deal."

CHAPTER 11

Pearls

Exhausted after my ordeal at the Wheel, I fell into a deep sleep. When I awoke, I was refreshed and able to continue my march away from the amusement park. After what seemed like just the right amount of time, I came upon a grove of Jacaranda trees in full bloom. Falling by the thousands, their blossoms released into the wind like tiny purple sparrows. On instinct, I hugged the trunk of the largest tree, shut my eyes, and thought about the Little Bridge.

When I opened them, I was back in The Garden by Aunt Betty, the green hammock hanging from her comforting branches. The Firemaker, her gown now a deep ruby red, was standing on a little bridge shaped like a crescent moon rising above a river of poppies. The air smelled faintly of roses and cinnamon, as it had when I first awoke in this place. And from somewhere unseen, the delicate tones of wind chime came softly into my awareness.

Before I met The Firemaker I would have been puzzled out of my mind at how this could be happening. Not anymore. What I would have described as strange had become normal. There was magic in this place and I was learning to be less afraid of what didn't make logical sense. I was thrilled to see The Firemaker again and walked toward the Little Bridge.

"Did you have an interesting time, Helen?"

"Yes, Firemaker, to say the least! It's not what I expected, though I don't know what I was expecting, actually."

"No, I suppose not. As I told you before, reality and fantasy aren't as different as one might imagine. Perhaps the First Door has helped you to begin to accept so-called *impossible* possibilities?"

"Yes, that's what's happening to me," I said laughing. "Impossible possibilities!"

"How do you feel about this journey now that you've been through the First Door? Will you be staying for more?"

I took a moment to see how I felt. It hadn't been easy so far, and my journey was just beginning. Doubts had started to kick in, but I knew what I wanted.

"I don't understand much of this, but what I experienced behind The First Door got my attention. So yes, Firemaker. I'd like to stay."

"Very good, Helen. Are you ready for the next door?"

"I think so, but there is this one small concern I just can't get past. I've asked you before. Do you mind if I ask again?"

"Not at all."

"Well, are you *sure* I'm not dead? I can take if I am; at least I think I can."

The Firemaker laughed. "You're not dead, Helen, I

"Okay, whew. Thank you! Just checking. This
pretty disturbing, and while I've got an opinion
what I saw, beyond that I don't know what I'm supposed ᴛᴏ ᴛᴀ
away from my experience behind the First Door."

"It'll come, Helen. It takes time to absorb all of this, but the
learning behind each door is learning you must have, no matter
what. You can do the work and acquire it now, or you can put
it off and acquire it later. But you can't really move on in any
significant way in your life without it."

"Move on, Firemaker?"

"Yes. Your understanding of how life works is *frozen,* so to
speak. Therefore, until you complete this course of learning, you
can't go on to the next level, and your life will continue to look
very much as it has in the past. Not a very satisfying place to be,
as I understand it."

"No, not satisfying at all," I said.

The Firemaker continued, "Not seeing more than you currently
see is actually a *choice.* It's a choice not to open to new perceptions
that will allow you to grow and understand so much more."

Instinctively, I knew she was right. I did want to grow and the
choice was mine to make. It was so elegantly simple.

"Thank you for explaining it to me, Firemaker."

She nodded and pointed west to the next door. "You understood
more than you know inside the First Door, Helen, and I think
what's up ahead will show you even more. Are you ready?"

"Yes, Firemaker, I am."

From some hidden pocket in her robe, she produced the little slip of paper from my fortune cookie.

"You threw this away. May I suggest you hang onto it? You never know. It could come in handy."

"Handy? I don't see how?"

"Anything that happens on this journey may be worth a second look. Suspend your fears and disbelief and be as conscious as you can, especially of your conclusions. I'll rejoin you soon."

I said goodbye to The Firemaker and left the Little Bridge, walking steadily west. The tile on the Second Door had a painting of a pearl—perfect, white, and radiant—nestled in its oyster shell. I leaned into the door, pushed it open and stepped through.

Amazed, more like horrified, I saw a large image of myself projected onto an enormous movie screen. Spellbound, I watched myself slipping down corridors of the past, gathering up my pain and sadness like shards of broken glass. I saw how over the years I'd gradually become more comfortable with my sadness than with joy, eventually nearly forgetting there were other ways to feel.

Sadness had become a sort of perverse inner companion, a symbol of my essence, or at least what I believed my essence to be.

Next, I saw my sadness transformed into an enchanted pearl. It hung from my neck, close to my heart. In some strange way I didn't comprehend, it made me feel different, as if I existed outside the parameters of the normal progression of people's lives, a solitary being waiting interminably for her life to begin.

The Pearl of Sadness had been with me for so long I could barely recall a time when it hadn't been there. The images on the screen began to show how the Pearl had formed – much like the grit that invades the oyster – from the cold, hard knot that had settled into the center of my chest so many years ago in childhood.

I'd never known how to get rid of my sadness and the pain that caused it. And though I thought I knew, I could see now that I'd never truly understood how it came to be or what purpose it had served in my life. Sadness had become the only feeling I recognized as my own, the only feeling that told me I was alive.

When the dark dreams came, and I couldn't remember who or where I was, Sadness let me know that I was still me. Still Helen. And that feeling, awful as it was, gave me something I could find safety in and count on to help me survive the night and endless days that followed.

Lost in thought, I suddenly became aware that I was not alone. Eyes focused upward, I hadn't noticed that I was standing unseen in an upper balcony high above an auditorium full of people. There were hundreds of them, as I would come to understand, all gathered to speak about their pain and bear witness to the sins and failures of their past.

"I'm an alcoholic!" shouted one.

"I hear you'," called out another. "I'm a survivor of child abuse!"

"Yeah, me too. And an overeater on top of it!" someone yelled from the back of the hall.

"That's a rough one!" another joined in, "Me, I'm codependent!"

"I'm this!" and "I'm that!" the people cried out to each other.

In a flash of knowing I realized that, *just like me,* their illnesses and injuries had become the foundation of their lives: They were naming themselves according to the particular wounds they'd suffered.

But instead of building on the things they loved and that brought them joy, they'd built upon sorrow and despair only to live on the soggy landfills of their past.

One by one, they came to the front of the auditorium, told their stories, claimed an identity, and were handed a pearl. As they returned to their seats, pearls in hand, they applauded and commiserated with one another, overjoyed at being recognized for their suffering and for their courage. They were proud of their pearls, and many had more than one.

In the dim light of the hall, the pearls glowed like snowflakes falling on a winter's night. Observing from the balcony, I saw the room was not unlike a sanctuary and the people were not unlike worshipers who caressed each other's pearls and prayed to their gods of pain.

My heart went out to them because I knew they didn't understand what they were doing. I hadn't realized I was doing it myself until a few moments ago. Just like them, my life had been spent pretending I was looking forward when all I could do was look back.

It was clear to me now that these pearls were a product of injury and struggle, nothing more than a coating smoothly formed around something sharp and foreign. We'd forgotten that it was our ability to transform the grit of life into something manageable that's the treasure; not the pearls formed in the process.

Certainly a pearl was a worthy symbol of all we'd endured and survived. Certainly discovering what was wrong and righting it was important, very important, but it wasn't the place to stop. It was the place to *start*.

Suddenly, my heart ached for these people, and for myself, and for the tiny prizes we'd settled for instead of real growth and true freedom.

As long as we confuse who we were *as people* with the Pearls we've created and for which we've paid so dearly, we'll never understand that, deep inside, no matter what happened to us in the past, we are all right.

Without this understanding, we keep on searching endlessly for some external something to protect us, to make us feel okay, not realizing that we're already whole. Our Pearls are simply proof of the process, not the process itself, much less a final resting point.

I couldn't stand it anymore and screamed out, "It's a mistake to confuse what happens *to us* with who we *are*! We're so much more than that! Please, please, *please!* SNAP OUT OF IT!"

No one batted an eye. They were oblivious to me and to my words.

It took a few moments to get my emotions under control and accept that they couldn't hear—or maybe wouldn't hear me. I don't know. Slowly, it dawned on me that they weren't ready to leave. I shrugged, my shoulders, turned, and headed for the nearest exit.

Pushing it open, I left and found my way back to The Garden. The sun was just coming up, and the sky was marmalade once again. I yawned and stretched, and then climbed into the hammock hanging beneath Aunt Betty's branches. As I did, the slip of paper from the fortune cookie fell out of my pocket.

I leaned down, picked it up and held it once more to the light. Now it read:

YOU ARE THE CREATOR, NOT THE PEARL

CHAPTER 12

Mists

"The Firemaker told me this was the place for change and it's that for sure."

I sat up and swung my legs over the side of the hammock. The Firemaker walking toward me, about twenty feet away on the Little Bridge.

"Have a nice rest, Helen?" she asked as I drew near.

"Yes, I feel great, all clear and refreshed!"

The Firemaker nodded. "Excellent, Helen. Any thoughts on your journey so far?"

"Absolutely. I think the Second Door was about self-fulfilling prophecies. At least, part of it was."

"It seems like everybody in that auditorium was sort of willing themselves into a small, stuck sort of life. That's not very thought through on my part, I know, but that's what it looked like to me."

"I see. Any insights about that regarding your own life?"

"Well yes, in some ways, that *is* the story of my life. And it's the story of a lot of other people I know. We get stuck and can't seem to move forward."

"Then, something comes along and propels us from wherever we are to the next place, usually against our will. That's a pretty rough way to get moved along."

"It can be. As I said before, while you're passing through the doors, it's important to be as aware as you can of the conclusions you make?"

"I remember," I said, nodding.

"I think you were trying to tell me to stand back from myself a bit and try to *watch* what I'm seeing and deciding."

"That's very good, Helen. Now I'll add a second point for you to consider. Leave room to imagine the possibility of *good* in what you see in the Land Behind the Doors, even if it appears to be negative at first."

"It does no good to judge yourself, the people in the Auditorium, or the people at the Wheel too harshly. First of all, you may not be seeing all there is to see because of your own preconceived attitudes and notions. They can color your conclusions."

She was right. And I knew it. My conclusions were about to be turned upside down.

"At The Wheel, did you notice the woman spinning for a new kidney for her friend, or the teacher spinning for books and supplies for her students?"

"In the Auditorium, did you see the gentleman who brought his daughter to demonstrate his remorse for hurting her with his drinking, or the young woman who wrote in her journal, 'I am free to choose what I do, and who I will be.' Did you notice any of that?"

I frantically searched my memory. "No, Firemaker. I didn't see them."

"They were there. And that's the problem with prejudging a situation. Because of old, ingrained preconceptions, you thought you understood. Everyone you noticed *seemed* to be greedy or foolish or stuck."

"It's an infinite universe. No one understands anything completely, at least not on the levels at which human beings presently exist."

"What you saw at The Wheel, and in the Auditorium, *was* disturbing, at least on the surface. But consider this, Helen. Isn't it better for a person to do whatever she must to begin healing than to deny she has a problem at all?"

"Yes, of course it is," I said, nodding my head in agreement. "They were probably saying and doing the best things they could to help themselves feel better. I'm the one who can't see. I'm the stupid one."

"You're not stupid, Helen. Far from it. You simply viewed the situation from the level at which you were *in at that moment.*"

"Sometimes it might not look like it, but for the most part, people are doing their best. Circumstances can make it extremely difficult for anyone, especially the person that is having the experience, to know with any real certainty what's actually happening."

"The people in the Auditorium were in the process of figuring out what meaning to attach to certain events in their lives. At the best of times, it's no small task to write the *true* story of one's Pearls."

"Many of the people you saw may not have been moving all that rapidly, but there are reasons for that. One of the most important is that choices are often made without the benefit of actual perspective. It's as if a mist obscures the way forward, the *Mists of Circumstance*."

"The Mists of Circumstance? I've never heard of it before. It sounds like some kind of fable. What does it mean, Firemaker?"

"It's real, Helen, though that doesn't mean it's not a fable. The Mists of Circumstance are made up of events, relationships and attitudes that combine to obscure our vision. It's like trying to peer through the fog when it's dark. It's nearly impossible to see in any direction or know with any certainty whether a choice will bring a good or bad outcome."

"So, what tends to happen is, shortly after making a decision, if things don't go immediately the way we'd hoped, we look back and think we must have been wrong, chosen poorly. It's a common thing to do. But as time passes, the mists lift and our vision clears, we often see that the choice we made was a good one."

I thought about that for a while. "You're right, Firemaker. When I look back at my decisions, I usually think I blew it. But sometimes, way down the road, I start to see that I did make the right choice after all. Unfortunately, Firemaker, until you're able to know if you've chosen wisely, the doubts just keep on coming."

The Firemaker nodded. "In time, Helen, as you move through the remaining doors, the Mists will begin to fall away. You'll see more clearly, and when it comes time to choose, you'll know what to do."

"Until then, simply knowing that the Mists exist and allowing for the difficulty of seeing through them will lessen your anxiety. And just as important, knowing this will free you from the heavy weight of judging others."

"Just like you, the people in the Auditorium fear that choices made recently or even long ago have ruined their lives. But to judge a choice without taking into consideration the Mists of Circumstance is to see only a very small part of the larger whole."

"It's a point of view that condemns any choice that was less than one hundred percent perfect, and that's an impossible standard."

"So, the next time you find yourself drawing hasty conclusions about a person's behavior, especially your own, consider the hidden reasons behind it, reasons you probably can't see, like pain or illness or fear. Those are the Mists of Circumstance and every person's will surely be different from yours."

"Someone may be struggling with something you're unable to see, much less understand, because it's an experience you've never had or cannot decipher."

"Here's something else to think about, and while it might at first be challenging to comprehend, in the end you may gain an interesting new perspective."

"If someone in desperate emotional pain chooses to drink heavily rather than to commit suicide, at least they're still alive."

"That means they still have the opportunity of change available to them. They still have a chance to continue to grow, past the heavy drinking."

"Isn't it better for a person, even if she's a hundred pounds overweight, to have another cookie than to give up on living? Because once the choice to give up is made, there can be no other."

I nodded and let her words sink in. "I think I get what you're saying, Firemaker. But don't people need limits? I mean, don't people overdo the handling of their pain by eating or taking drugs or spending too much money, you know, anything that might help them escape their pain for a while?"

"And what about going so far that you hurt somebody else? The kind of stuff you're talking about tends to get people into a lot of trouble."

"It seems to me that most of the people I saw in the Auditorium were there because they, or someone close to them, had been doing too much of something in order to avoid pain in real time."

The Firemaker nodded. "Of course. It only makes sense to recognize the potential for self-abuse that can grow from pain. And you are correct to be concerned about the damage that comes to others from self-abuse."

"What I'm talking about is someone in a truly desperate state of mind, a mind so filled with anguish it cannot take another moment of pain – another moment of life. To turn to something else, even though that something else might eventually cause more anguish, is still to choose life over death."

"I know that runs counter to everything you've been told about what it means to be strong, but how many people simply weren't able to face another day without relief, even relief that comes from a questionable source? Are they better off dead?"

"What I'm telling you is that, when a person chooses life, she's choosing the possibility of growth, change, and right action. Consider this: The homeless panhandler you see passed out on the street today may save a child's life tomorrow."

"In every individual, in every moment, there exists the potential to become something greater, to evolve, to truly recover and know that they are whole. But all of that is negated if the choice is death."

The Firemaker paused to let her words sink in. "Let me tell you a little story, Helen. I think you'll find it interesting and quite educational."

CHAPTER 13

The City of Joy

"As the story begins, let's say that you and some friends have just learned that a place called the City of Joy exists somewhere beyond the horizon. It's a place of peace, happiness and beauty."

"You talk it over and, in time, put together a caravan and set out to find that marvelous place. Why wouldn't you? It would be madness *not* to want to live in such a place."

"So, all your provisions are gathered, your maps obtained, transportation is arranged and you set out. At first, things go well and everyone is in great spirits."

"But along the way, quite unexpectedly you enter a place called the Terrible Desert. None of the maps showed this challenging place, so you find yourselves completely unprepared."

"In the Terrible Desert, you're assaulted by bandits and ravaged by sandstorms. There's no fresh water, and you think you'll die from the sweltering heat. Soon, the caravan comes to a complete stop. You're stuck. Stranded."

"Weeks pass with scant food, water and shelter, and you despair of ever getting out alive, much less of finding the City of Joy. In fact, the City of Joy is the last thing on your mind. You just want out of this terrible place and into any place that's better."

"Fortunately, just in time, another caravan comes along, heading for a place of safety. These travelers were once in exactly the same straits as you, but somehow managed to make it out, get back on their feet, and find a decent, safe place to call home, the City of Stability."

"Because they learned many a hard lesson and took it to heart, they've become able to pass through the Terrible Desert safely. They know what to look out for in themselves and the environment. They know where the water is, where the bandits hide and where the quicksand lies."

"And, they know that as long as certain rules are adhered to and the path that got them out before is followed, the odds are very good they'll never be stranded in the Terrible Desert again."

"I think I'm starting to get it."

"Good," said The Firemaker. "Now, let's say that your caravan joins the caravan that knows the way to the City of Stability, and with some real effort and the help of those who have been there before, you all make it to this place safely. Naturally, you're relieved to be out of the madness, danger and despair. You're elated simply to be safe and fed and warm."

"Who does that remind you of, Helen?"

"Me, in Peri's garden. And the people in the Auditorium?"

"That's right. So, to return to the story, of course you're ecstatic to be in the City of Stability. For a while, maybe a *long* while, you're content to repeatedly discuss and relive the difficulties and challenges you overcame in the Terrible Desert. Recounting the horrors gives you comfort and a way to release the fears."

"It also helps you to feel empowered when you remember that it was once *very* bad and now it's much better. Even more important, it's wonderful to realize that you've stopped the blind wandering and that things are so much better largely because of your own intelligent efforts. It makes sense to gather together with others of similar experience and share all that."

"And that's what admiring each other's Pearls is all about."

"Yes, and to judge that harshly is to deny people their joy, power and self-direction."

"Even so, there almost inevitably comes a time when you begin to long for *more* than stability. Stability is important, certainly, but it doesn't usually nurture the parts of us that are the most inventive and alive. You find you miss being creative. But creativity isn't encouraged in the City of Stability."

"In fact, if you get too creative, the 'Old Masters' of Stability – those who've been there the longest and who've decided that where they are is good enough for *everyone* – may sternly warn you off becoming too bold. They may even tell you that you risk being thrust back into the Terrible Desert if you don't calm down and worship your hard-won Pearl like a good girl."

"But just being stable isn't why you were put on this earth. You weren't born just to put out negative fires and dwell on past victories. You're here to light new fires of creativity all your own. And that's the impulse, the drive that makes you begin to hunger once more for the City of Joy."

"Yes, I'm beginning to understand a little of that, to long for that. But if I ache so much to move forward, then why am I still stuck in the City of Stability? In fact, why don't *all* of us just go for it?"

"Many reasons, Helen. There's the fear of old disasters revisiting you and the fear of new demons you may not be able to recognize. There's a reluctance to let go of stale relationships and the fear of taking risks. And many other reasons, too."

"But eventually, despite their fears, most people will press on toward the City of Joy. It's as inevitable an impulse as the one that some birds feel in migration. It's built in to all of us to desire to grow, to rise, level by level, until we reach our final destination."

"And this journey you're on, traversing the Land Behind the Doors, means you've left the City of Stability and are again seeking the City of Joy, just like you sought a piece of sun as a little girl. The two pursuits are the same, and that's what you're doing right now."

As The Firemaker told the story, I began to understand more about myself and my experiences behind the Doors. It was as if something that had been all knotted up for a long time gently began to untangle. It felt good, and yet there was something troubling me.

"Firemaker, what about the people who spend their whole lives stuck, doing the same things over and over and over again? I mean, why doesn't the Universe just kick us out of the Auditorium so we'll get on with it?"

The Firemaker laughed. "Well, Helen," she said, "in spite of what you may have been told, the Infinite Intelligence that created the Universe isn't the least bit concerned with how long you sit around in the Auditorium admiring your Pearls. Not the least bit."

"But how can that be?"

"Things are set up that way because what you want matters, especially to *you*. And the Universe respects that. You see, you have been set free on the path of exploration to exercise your personal will. Otherwise, you'd be little more than a robot."

"Sooner or later, no matter who you are, you will eventually sense that for maximum growth it's far better to remove the Pearl, the negative past, all of it, from the center of your consciousness."

"Otherwise, you'll just keep building a bigger and bigger Pearl all your life. And there's such a thing as a Pearl that's become too heavy to carry, a Pearl that's too large to circumnavigate. In fact, circumnavigation is a good way to remember this lesson."

"Once, the idea that the world was flat was a large collective Pearl in human consciousness, so much so, for all intents and purposes, the world *was* flat. For most of human history, no one could circumnavigate such an enormous Pearl or even begin to conceive of the idea that the world might be round and could be..."

"Circumnavigated! I understand!! You're saying the Pearl is really a temporary stop, a way station along the greater journey of a person's life, or our collective lives as human beings, right?"

"Very good, Helen. And, because it's built into human beings to keep progressing, your own boredom or impatience with staying at the Pearl level will sooner or later put you back on the path, seeking to solve the greater problem."

"Which is..." I said slowly, "to pass through the Auditorium dedicated to the Pearls of the Past and remove the Pearl from your life once and for all?"

"Exactly. And to do that, you have to move forward and smash the Pearl altogether. It's the only way to be rid of it, and ultimately, nothing less will do."

"There's nothing sadder than the person who lives her life in the good old days and never moves on to the good *new* days based on who and what she is in the present."

"But Firemaker, I don't know how to smash my Pearls."

"Not yet, but if you continue this journey, soon you will. Until then, I can tell you that since the pain goes *on* in layers, it must come *off* in layers, too. That process must continue until the Pearl becomes a size that's manageable – and then you can smash it and be done with it once and for all."

The Firemaker paused. "But I think that's enough for now about Pearls and a flat earth. I believe you're anxious to go through the next door."

As usual, it was all a bit overwhelming, but I wanted to go on, so I shook the dizziness from my head and, with a smile and a nod, told her "I'm ready."

CHAPTER 14

The Third Door

Outside the Third Door, I paused and looked carefully at the tile. One of Peri's nieces had painted it with a honeybee circling a yellow daisy, and in the background, a beehive. It was pretty and I paused to touch it. After a moment, I pushed the door open and stepped through...

The broken branches of a fallen Morton Fig exposed the inner rings of its giant trunk. These rings, the ones that form inside the heart of a tree for each year of living, map the tree's life. And if you study them, you can learn what the tree survived -- drought, disease, and so on. Kind of like scars, they tell the story of each particular tree's experience.

With only the remains of the great Morton to welcome me, I was feeling uncomfortable, and just a little sad. But I had a purpose, and so I began to scan the area for something to guide my next steps. It took a while, but eventually I found what I needed, a sign for travelers like me no doubt. Crudely painted with small print, it read, simply:

KEEP GOING

There was an arrow, too, and it pointed in the direction of a nearby dirt road. Relieved to be on my way, I set out. After an hour, maybe more, the road began to narrow and gradually thin into almost no road at all, little more than an animal track or hunting trail. The feeling that I was walking further away from any place I'd wanted to be was strong and I thought it might be wise to consult The Firemaker. "What do I do, Firemaker? This place doesn't feel right."

I was still making my way behind this door so I wasn't surprised when there was no response and continued walking. Once sunlit, the fields had grown dense and ominous, just like the rapidly darkening sky.

From not far ahead, where the trail narrowed even more, and Cottonwood trees grew so densely I feared becoming lost, came a droning noise that at first I mistook for some kind of machine. Whatever it was made the hair on the back of my neck stand up. With great caution, I kept moving, even as the sound grew louder and louder as I came into an especially densely wooded area.

There, right in middle of the trail, seven or eight feet tall and swarming with bees, was the biggest, scariest, baddest beehive I'd ever seen. I froze. How could I get around this thing? Then it hit me, maybe getting around it wasn't as important as getting away from it, so I retreated and climbed onto a nearby rock under the branches of a Live Oak that looked an awful lot like Aunt Betty.

Heart squeezing, my mind tumbling with fear, I knew I could not keep on. "I can't go ahead with the Mother of All Beehives in the way. I suppose I could go back the way I came. Or I could try to go around the woods, but who knows how far it is or how long it'd take?!"

Then it hit me. I didn't know where I was going. For all I knew, maybe I was already there! As I considered my predicament, I caught a swift movement out of the corner of my eye. A woman ran down the trail past me toward the hive. Unbelievable as it sounds, she was naked but for the mascara that ran down her face as she cried out, "I need the honey! I need it now!"

I nearly fell off my perch. She was in for some serious trouble. Regaining my composure, I called out to her, "Lady! Wait! There's a humongous beehive with a gazillion bees up ahead, and you're as naked as a newborn babe! They'll sting you like crazy!"

Heedless of my warning and heedless of the bees, she sped toward the hive, body exposed, arms outstretched, hands held high as if the rainbow's end were up ahead.

Our eyes met for a split second as she passed and shouted, "Mind your own business, you stupid girl!"

I couldn't watch anymore and hunkered down, burying my face into my knees. "Oooh! This is gonna be nasty."

Sure enough, a couple of seconds later, she came running out from the hive screaming in pain and covered with bees, hundreds more following in deadly pursuit. I was so frightened I hid behind the tree just in case the bees decided to go after me. But I could still see what was happening. The woman was in agony. And though I hadn't been stung, I felt horrible and my body cramped with pain. I will never forget the confused expression on her tormented face as she fled up the long trail and out of sight, yelling over and over, "Why?! Why?!"

Unable to utter a word, I could only stand very still and wait. Minutes passed and The Firemaker had still not appeared. I had no idea what I should do. But that was okay for the moment because I needed a little time to pull myself together.

There would be no recovery. Another woman was on her way down the trail. At least she was wearing something – thank God! Bare limbed, with only a summer shift to cover her body, she'd taken a few precautionary measures. In sunglasses and hiking boots, she twirled and jabbed a toy sword about, making wide, loopy circles in the air as she strode purposefully toward the hive.

"Not another one!" I groaned. "This is unbelievable!" I had to warn her. "Lady! LADY! Wait a second! There's a giant beehive up ahead. I just saw another woman..."

But just as before, this woman paid no attention. I tried several more times to get her to stop, but she would have none of me and continued on her way straight into the hive.

"I know what I'm doing, you silly girl!" she yelled as she passed by. But only moments later, there she was, running out screaming, swatting at a cloud of bees as they stung every exposed part of her body.

"*Why* would they hurt me like this?" she cried with a voice more feral than human, and then vanished down the trail.

Once again I sought safety behind the tree. Stunned and sickened by the unfathomable foolishness I'd just seen, I stayed close to the Live Oak, waiting for the bad feelings to go away.

As I rode it out, it occurred to me that I didn't know, couldn't know, what those women were feeling that could have caused them to behave so recklessly. The Firemaker had cautioned me not to judge too quickly, and for once I was doing things right.

Perhaps these women were simply misguided, not silly or stupid, as I'd first thought. Perhaps they were wearing Pearls of Pain so big they'd become blinded to the danger of bees, let alone an entire hive of them?

"How are you doing, little lady?" someone said.

Very carefully I peeked out from behind the tree.

"I—I—I'm fine, thank you. Who are you?"

"I'm the beekeeper and that's my hive down the road there." The beekeeper pointed through the smoke that was billowing from an iron pot she carried, every inch of her protected by bulky layers of a special, impenetrable suit.

"Name's Helen," I said, stepping closer to get a look at her equipment. "Isn't your suit uncomfortable?"

"Not nearly as uncomfortable as a few hundred bee stings! Anyway, I've been at this so long I hardly notice the suit anymore. Wouldn't go near the hive without it."

"Well, I've been sitting here watching people run naked and half naked over to the hive like it was a tea party or something. I tried to warn them but they went anyway.

The beekeeper snorted, "I see it all the time. Just about nobody wants to listen anymore. There's no point trying to get people to protect themselves if they won't listen."

"Have you ever been stung?"

"Several times," I nodded. It's not a very nice experience."

"Nope. And unlike a lot of things that toughen you up, this only gets worse. No immunity from it if it happens too many times. After awhile, if you've been stung often enough, it only takes one sting to make you really sick.

"It's like an allergy, you know? You become allergic to the poison and when that happens, well, one sting is as strong as a hundred. It even kills some folks."

"I've heard that."

"Yep. But you can't blame it on the bees. They make honey and they sting. That's just a part of what bees do. People want the honey and they think they can just ignore the stings. Never works." She shook her head sadly. "Nope, never works."

"Well, I gotta get to work. You take care, Helen."

"Wait a minute!" I called out to her as she walked toward the bees. "Can you tell me how to get past the beehive?"

"Getcha a suit!" she said over her shoulder without stopping.

"But where—how do I—?"

Too late. The beekeeper was on the other side of the hive, already deep into her work. I was alone again, my questions trailing without answer. I didn't know what to do, which didn't feel very good. But then I remembered the pouch. Lifting it from around my neck I quickly opened it, hoping to find some of The Firemaker's promised good luck.

I pulled out a gold coin with an inscription of the word *Inside*. And on the other was written, *Belief Plus Action Is How We Create and Creation Is What You're Here To Do.*

Still dazed and deeply unsettled by what I'd seen, I could only stand there and look at the coin, turning it over again and again in my hand. Finally, I pulled myself together, stuck the coin back in the pouch, put the string around my neck, and stood up.

"This is getting me nowhere. Clearly my only choice is to backtrack." So I walked out the way I'd gone in, glad to leave the sound of the hive behind me.

I made slow progress and couldn't put the coin out of my mind. So much so that my thoughts turned into a little chant... *inside I go to seek what I believe!*

What I'd seen at the Beehive left me so rattled, my aching head exploded into a full-blown migraine.

"Fine! I get it! Enough!" I sobbed, heat pouring from my eyes, shooting fire.

If belief plus action is how we create and creation is what we're here to do, how about this? *"I BELIEVE. I WANT. TO CREATE. A WAY. OUT. OF HERE. NOW!!!"*

At my breaking point I reached for a rock, throwing it against a pot of smoke the Beekeeper left behind. *Ka-thunk!* "How's *that* for action?!" I yelled, dizzy, sick, and a tiny bit relieved.

My swing must have had some velocity because I stumbled backwards and fell over a large bush, landing on my bottom.

CHAPTER 15

The People in the Beehive

Apparently I'd shifted something in a big way because when I finally looked up I was back in The Garden sitting under the sheltering branches of Aunt Betty. The Firemaker was only a few feet away on the Little Bridge, enjoying a nice chuckle at my expense.

"That was beautiful work, Helen. You're starting to get the hang of this and I'm proud of you."

I got up, rubbing my backside as I picked twigs out of my hair and walked to meet her. "Thank you, but I didn't do anything except have a tantrum, throw a rock and fall down."

"Well, in truth you rarely know exactly which action is the one that'll do the trick. Sometimes you have to make a lot of noise and thunder like you just did to get the attention of a helper—such as myself."

"I helped you out a little on that one because you'd been at the Beehive long enough. It was time for you to leave, and for us to discuss your observations and move on to the next door."

"Usually you won't get results like that so quickly and easily, at least not at first."

"But now you know the way and you can do it again when the time comes again. You stated what you wanted, Helen, and you sincerely meant it. Then you took an action, even if it didn't seem directly related to what you wanted."

"That's true, but I've said things and meant them before, and I've even taken action, but I didn't get instant results, at least not good ones."

"As I said, you'll rarely know exactly what triggered the response you were hoping for. The point is to go on believing, and keep adding to the stack of actions you're building."

"You're in direct contact with me now and can ask for help, and you're gaining more and more power on your own."

"In this situation, you suspended judgment, demanded a way out, and I helped. This was a minor demand and of little overall consequence to your life, and now you've had a demonstration of how belief plus action works."

"If it had been something that ran against your greatest good, I couldn't have helped you, but that wasn't the case here."

"You haven't mastered the process, and you'll have plenty of misfires, but you're on your way. Now tell me, how did you find the experience of the Third Door?"

"It seemed like a dead end to me, no pun intended. Complete and utter madness. There was a naked woman, a half-naked woman, a giant beehive, and a woman in a protective suit."

"I'm *sooooo* confused, Firemaker. What does it all mean?"

The Firemaker said gently, "Tell me about your family, Helen."

"My family? Hmmm. Well, there's nothing much to tell. I have virtually no contact with any of them and haven't for many years. Why do you ask?"

"Do you miss them?"

"Yes, and no. I've always wished that it could be different than it was, maybe the ability to be together without all the fighting and anger that went on when I was living at home."

"So you long for the sweetness, the *idea* of family, yet you never call or visit them. Correct?"

"Oh, I've gone by my parents' house a time or two over the years when my brothers were all there for Thanksgiving or something."

"But it's always the same as it ever was. Nastiness breaks out and ruins everything, and then I feel sick for days, sometimes much longer. So, I guess what you said is essentially correct. I just about never call or visit. Not any more."

"Can you tell me why you keep your distance?"

"Because it's too painful to be near them. I always get hurt. The truth is, and I feel sort of extreme for saying this, deep down I don't feel safe. There's always this jolt of fear that shoots through my spine, and no matter what I do or how hard I try, I can't shake it."

"So what would you say this door is about, Helen?"

"I don't have the faintest—wait a minute! My *family* is the Beehive?"

"Yes, as is any relationship, consumption or habit that repeatedly hurts you. You tell yourself there's something sweet in there, but something stronger warns you that the price is too high or perhaps the sweetness isn't really there at all."

"The Beehive represents *any* connection you have that damages you again and again. It could be your family, a job, a lover, a friend, but the principle is the same. Do you see?"

I must have turned a little green or something because The Firemaker asked me how I was feeling.

"A little light headed, maybe."

"Is that the feeling you had as you watched the women go toward the hive?"

"Yeah, I felt sick all over."

"Like you'd been stung?"

"Me? Well, nothing happened to me. They're the ones who got hurt!"

"Yes. They went in believing they could change the nature of the situation, or at least handle it, and they got stung."

"Look at how you're feeling now, Helen. Though indirectly, you were stung, too."

"You were trying to keep them from doing something incredibly foolish and dangerous. But their reaction essentially was 'How dare you try to keep me from getting stung? I'll sting YOU for that! 'And so they did, verbally."

"If you had told them they had hurt you with their words, it's very likely they'd have stung you *again* for even suggesting that they sting other people with their words and actions."

"Yes, you were stung, and that's why you feel so ill. It's not a judgment, only an observation."

"You're right, Firemaker. I thought I felt bad because it hurt to see them hurt. But it was more than that. I was physically ill, dizzy and sick to my stomach. I had to put my head down and rest."

"Being stung is much more than merely an unnerving experience. It's painful and disorienting and, as the beekeeper told you, it never gets any less so, no matter how many times it happens."

My brain was fast approaching overload. My whole notion of those women as victims and of myself as a victim had just been turned upside down.

Sure, they were injured at the hive, just as I'd been bruised and battered every time I attempted to go back to those dangerous places I thought held the sweetness I craved so badly.

But if I understood The Firemaker correctly, that was only part of the lesson of this door. There was also the lesson that those women—all of us—do plenty of stinging, too, and most of the time without even knowing it.

"So you're saying that in one way or another, we're virtually *all* Stingers?"

The Firemaker answered, "Not all. Not people who have become aware of these concepts and incorporated them into their lives."

"What I *am* saying is that if one is not careful, it's very easy to sting other people out of some misguided sense of self-defense."

"Being defensive and hurtful when *anyone* tries to help by suggesting an alternative way of behaving is simply to choose a path that will result in lost ground in one's progress."

"Okay, I see that. But there must be a way out of this madness. If belief plus action is how we create, and creation is what we're here to do, then what I believe and how I act in relation to the situation determines what I'm able to create, right?"

"You're getting close, Helen. A few doors from now you'll understand much more about how the Law of Creation functions."

"For the time being, your interpretation will serve you. Just understand that it's a guiding force for all human beings, whether they know it or not."

"What about this, Firemaker? In a Beehive situation, I believe two things: one, that there's sweetness in the hive that I long for, and two, that it's not worth getting hurt over."

"Yes, that's how it seems, but thinking there's sweetness in the hive is not your genuine belief. Your genuine belief is that there is no sweetness in there, and even if there were, the price is too high."

"And that's how your life actually is. You don't have contact with the Beehive, your family, because you don't truly believe that sweetness exists there. As a result, you've concluded that abstinence from them is the only safe way to proceed."

"But what about those women who got stung, Firemaker? Didn't they believe in what they were doing? They certainly *looked* like it going in. Why did it end so badly if they were so sure of themselves?"

"In spite of appearances, deep inside, where their true beliefs reside, they knew what they were in for. But they overrode those beliefs and past experiences at the Beehive because they simply would not accept that bees have two natures, one to produce sweetness and the other to sting, and they paid a price for ignoring one of those facts."

"In most cases people know they're Stingers, as you call them, in spite of what they tell themselves to the contrary. The most effective way to keep your myths alive is to surround yourself with other people whose beliefs and actions are based on those same myths."

"Stingers don't look like Stingers to other Stingers. Or at least their behavior doesn't seem out of the ordinary or offensive and dangerous to other people who're using the same tactics."

"You've seen pictures of beekeepers completely covered by bees and yet they're not stung. Why do you think that happens?"

"I guess it's because they aren't pretending that the bees won't sting them. Somehow they've learned how to go near the bees, and even be covered by them and not get stung. And since they actually know it and believe it, that's how it comes out."

"Excellent, Helen. That's it exactly."

"Okay, I'm good with that then. But Firemaker, can you tell me who those women were? I felt like I knew them somehow, and the beekeeper, too."

"All versions of you during different phases of your life."

"The first woman was you, naked and innocent, full of need, blindly rushing in."

"The second was you, too, but a bit smarter, a bit more aware, yet still attacking the situation with the wrong tools."

"Finally, the beekeeper represented you completely protected and full of knowing about the dual nature of the bees, or in this case, your own family."

"Ah, yes. Now I get it. Bees may make honey, but they also sting. So, either stay away from the hive or tell yourself the truth and be fully protected before you go in. Right?"

"Right. And?"

"And there may or may not be honey there in the first place."

"And?"

"Let me see. I'll bet I could find the honey or something just as sweet somewhere else without going through all that agony. I could go where there's honey readily available, but no bees and no hive. No beekeeper suit necessary."

"And, best of all, no stings, not by anyone, me included. But where do I find such a place?"

"The coin, Helen, think of the coin."

My mind flashed to the coin.

"Inside," I whispered, "Inside."

CHAPTER 16

Broken Maps

The Firemaker nodded, "Yes, Helen. Inside. All the sweetness of life, all you could ever imagine or want, is right inside of you."

"But it's not how I *feel*, Firemaker. I don't feel all sweet inside."

"Not yet. You're still carrying a burden that must be put down. Those sad feelings aren't really what's at the center of you. The feeling that they are is a trick of your ego, like a bad map that keeps leading you astray."

"But you're learning and you'll find your way if you just keep opening new doors. Are you ready to continue, or do you need to rest?"

"No more rest, Firemaker. I've had it with rest. I want what's mine. I want *me,* free and clear, happy and sweet and full of love. I can have that, can't I? That's what this is all about, isn't it?"

"Yes, Helen, all that's true. Ready for the next door, then?"

"To the next door. Let's do it!"

The Firemaker motioned to the Fourth Door. Its tile had been painted with a picture of a piece of pie. I smiled. There was no quitting now. I leaned my weight into the door, pushing it open. "I can do this. I can get through every last door."

CHAPTER 17

The Fourth Door

The door gave way easily. With a whoosh and a stumble, I found myself inside the entrance of a Fifties-style diner. A revolving door was at my back and, tucked up against both sides of the long narrow room, twin rows of cherry red booths beckoned me to come in.

I looked around for a few seconds, found the closest empty booth and plopped down. Without asking if I wanted anything, a waitress slid up next to the booth, turned the white coffee cup upright and said, "Take cream with your coffee, honey?"

"Sure. Um, well, actually, do you have tea?" Too late. My cup was already filled to the brim with hot coffee.

"Be right back with a menu, kid," she said, as she darted away, gliding into the kitchen on slick linoleum floors.

Almost as suddenly as she'd gone, she was back, flopping down a menu. I ordered a piece of banana cream pie as she pushed a dish of those little plastic pots of cream my way. You know the kind. Those little white buckets with flat, peel-off lids found in every inexpensive diner and café in the world? Right, those.

It wasn't long before I knew what this door was about. The waitress grinned and got right to the point, "Ever had any of that sweetheart trouble, honey?"

"Oh, that. Yeah, I sure have. A truckload. Does it show?" I mumbled.

"Well, it's always that or money. Most everybody who passes through the diner's got problems with one or the other."

A smile sent her weathered face into a thousand lines as she darted away to fetch my pie.

"Excuse me, could you make that *two* pieces of pie, please?"

"Sure thing, honey!"

She was back in a flash and we took up the conversation as if she'd never left.

"I guess you know all about bad relationships then," I said, digging my fork into the pie.

"More than a little, honey, more than a little. Why don't you tell me your version?"

"The standard cliché. My relationships have been pretty disappointing, to understate it by a million percent. In the beginning they're hypnotic and full of fireworks, but in the end they all seem to die a painful death. And unless I'm completely to blame every single time, I couldn't tell you why."

The waitress pushed the dish with the pots of cream closer to me, listening without comment.

"It's funny you bring this up because I'd kind of just shoved *that* challenge onto the back burner. But when I think about it, my love life is a mess. No sooner am I out of one relationship then I forget how uncomfortable it was and start dreaming about how wonderful it would be to meet someone new."

"That's understandable. Romantic love: Sweet as honey, but dangerous as a swarm of bees sometimes, right?"

"Oh, so you know about the Beehive and all of that?" I asked.

Before she could answer, a flurry of foul language came from the kitchen. Flashing a quick smile, the waitress hollered back, "You'd better not be fryin' eggs back there, Rae. And don't you bark at me, either! I told you the customer wants 'em poached. It's not my fault nobody likes 'em fried anymore."

"Rae's old fashioned. Only way she knows to cook is to drop the food in hot grease and stand back until it catches fire." She casually rested her right hand against the tabletop and grinned at me again, as if exchanging insults with the cook was as much a part of her day as putting on makeup.

"About the Beehive, yeah, I know about that. I work in the Land Behind the Doors, kiddo. You pick things up."

"I guess so," I said, a bit uncertainly. "I really hadn't thought about it until now. But that Third Door wasn't just about family, it had a lot to tell me about my love relationships, too."

I swallowed another mouthful of pie. "You know, I really try to make these things work, and that's the honest truth. But something always goes wrong, and one of us becomes unhappy, and soon we're *both* unhappy, and then we're finished."

"Sometimes being a couple ain't all it's cracked up to be. Mind if I sit? I'm on my break."

Without waiting for an answer, she slid into the seat across from me. "Look here, I'll show you something that might help. See these, whatever you call them, these little pots of cream?" She held up one of the small plastic cream containers.

"Imagine that one of these pots of cream is a person." She set the little bucket down on its base.

"Now, take another pot from the dish and stand it on its little flat head on top of that first one. Follow me, honey?"

I did as she said and stacked the two containers, top-to-top with one right side up and the other upside down. "Like this?"

"That's it. See, when you put them together the stack looks almost solid, right?"

I nodded.

"From the outside, it pretty much looks like one thing, one whole unit, doesn't it? And if you got used to seeing the pots of cream linked up like that, pretty soon you'd think they came that way, like that's how they're supposed to look. You'd begin to think that one pot of cream alone is only half of what it ought to be."

"Uh-huh, I get it."

"Well, most people don't get that, at least not at first, if they ever do. And that's the problem. The individuals in relationships can become like these two pots of cream."

"From the outside they look like one unit, and all the single pots of cream, the single people, are so busy thinking how wonderful the joined-up units have it they don't notice that one pot is sitting on top of the other."

"All kinds of unpleasant stuff can happen in a situation like that. I mean when you've got two people getting together just so they won't feel like they're incomplete."

I nodded.

"So like most people, you fight with your sweetie from time to time, I imagine?"

"Oh, certainly. Some more than others. There were at least a few I wish I'd never met. It's a funny thing, though, because most of them turned out to be versions of the same person, only with a different face, different body, and a different set of circumstances. It's almost as if they were a series of prototypes. In fact, sometimes I just call them my *Protos*. It simplifies things and puts the confusion on me. I chose them after all, so there must be something in me that keeps picking the same type."

The waitress grinned, then laughed out loud. "*Protos* huh? I like that!"

I nodded and continued. "Don't get me wrong, I'm not saying they were bad people or anything. I've been in love, and the rest of them, well there were a few I really cared for, you know? I even came close a couple of times to finding that permanent sweet spot everybody longs for, but it never stayed sweet long enough."

By this time, even though I'm not a coffee drinker, I'd emptied a packet of sugar and a couple of those little gizmos of cream into my cup and drained it, scarfed down the rest of my pie and was well into the second piece.

"Like I was saying, it wasn't all bad. I wouldn't want you to think that," I said, with a mouth full of pie.

"I learned something about myself each time, about what I wanted and all. And there were good times, laughs and hugs along the way, too. Anyway, it's in the past. I'm over it, more or less."

"Except for *one*. I thought, this is the *one*! But, as it turned out, that one was darned near the end of me. Probably thought the same thing about me, too."

I finished the pie, pushed my empty plate away and said, "Just like the others, it went sour right before my eyes. Suddenly we were done, and I was in the revolving door again. It took me a long time to accept that we were over."

I was on a roll. The caffeine, sugar, and talk about love gone wrong had seriously loosened my tongue. Before I was finished I'd slogged through two more cups of coffee and my entire Rolodex of lost loves, near misses and absolute screw-ups.

"I should be wearing a tee shirt," I groaned, rubbing my bloated belly, "with a big broken heart on it that says, 'Unlucky in Proto Land'."

That was meant to be funny, but for some reason, my eyes welled up with tears.

"Here," the waitress said, pulling a hankie from her sleeve.

I dabbed my tears and wrapped up with, "You know, once it's all over, the reasons don't seem so important. But I still remember the way it felt when everything started to go wrong."

"It's as if I was compelled to defend myself against something in the relationship, even if I didn't know what it was. I felt that if

I didn't stand up for myself, what *I* wanted was going to go the way of the dinosaurs, you know, vanish altogether."

"That's okay kid. We've all got our own love lament."

"But I'll tell you this much, what you're describing, that nagging feeling you couldn't put your finger on, well, that's what happens when you get into one of those stacked-up relationships. Shoot, girl, it's usually not even personal. It's really about logistics."

"The one on the bottom struggles to get on top while the one on top struggles to stay there. It shouldn't be a battle for supremacy, of course. But once you're in a stacked-up deal, it's obviously a whole lot better to be the one on top than the one on the bottom. Well, unless the bottom is where you want to be." She squinted, pulling a cigarette from her apron.

"You know, even when it wasn't so bad, I always felt a kind of subtle jockeying for position going on, a kind of unspoken competition. Half the time I thought I was imagining it, or that something was wrong with me because I didn't know how to get along."

"Well, I don't know you personally, so I couldn't say if anything's wrong with you or not. Doesn't look like it from here. But what you're describing is how it is for lots of folks. Stacked up and messed up," she said, taking a drag from what I could now see was actually an e-cigarette.

"Old habit," she said as she leaned back in the seat with a flick of her wrist at the ashtray next to the napkin holder. "Its not on."

With a wink she shoved it back into her apron and continued. "You've probably seen some stacked-up relationships where the same person always ends up getting hurt. You know, where the one on top stays on top and the one on the bottom stays on the bottom *all the time,* right? What a deal, huh? Be glad you're not in one of those."

"Oh, believe me, I am. But truthfully, that doesn't make me feel any better. I still want a partner in life. A good one."

"Well, don't give up, honey," the waitress said. She took the top pot of cream off the other one and placed it on the table, side-by-side with the first.

"It can also be like this," she said with surprising tenderness. "See, each pot of cream is already full but people just forget that they're full and that in reality *nobody* else can fill them up. Getting that concept wrong is a fast way to ending up with another pot of cream sitting on your head."

I looked at the waitress and studied her face for the first time. It was deeply lined with her living underneath the gaiety of her makeup. Clearly, she was speaking from experience.

She wore her hair in a beehive up-do and a small pink nameplate with "SUGAR" on it pinned to her blouse. I smiled at the perfection of it all as a sudden burst of affection and familiarity welled up inside me. It was as if I'd started every morning with breakfast in this diner and Sugar as my waitress my whole adult life.

"I'm sorry. How rude of me. We've been talking all this time and I haven't even introduced myself. I'm Helen."

Sugar offered her hand, "I'm Sugar. I guess that's pretty obvious," she said, pointing to her blouse. "Nice to meet you, Helen."

"Likewise," I said.

"Lemme show you something else, kiddo." Sugar pushed the two pots of cream together until they touched each other. "See that? Now that's a pretty thing. Each one is just exactly as important as the other, worth the same and holding the same amount of goodness."

"Being in a stacked-up relationship is worse than no relationship at all, if you ask me. But if you can get to this place, touching each other softly in this way, yet still equal at the base, then you've got something worthwhile."

"I know it can be hard to stop the cycle. After all, romantic love can work on you just like a drug. At first it makes you feel fantastic. But the high wears off, and if things go bad, you're like a junkie without the fix. I think you get my point."

"The trick is, just try not to grab for romantic love like a life preserver every time the circumstances in your life change and you start feeling lonely or scared 'cause you think you're only half full."

CHAPTER 18

Leaving Rooms

Just then, several people met at the door to the diner with one group leaving as another group came in. They bunched up, facing each other and did that side-to-side thing where both sides guess wrong about which way the other is going and it looks like a kind of goofy little dance.

Finally, everybody laughed, sorted it out, and the "leavers" left and the "enterers" entered.

Sugar said, "That little cha-cha over at the door just now, you saw that, right? That group of folks going out and the other group coming in?"

"Sure, happens all the time," I said.

"Sure does and in more ways than one. That's a good illustration of what we've been talking about. You meet people and hit it off for a while, things go great, then after a bit, you find them boring or in some cases, you can barely stand each other."

"Quite the mystery. What's behind that anyway, Sugar?"

"Well, it's like those people at the door just now. Some were coming into this room while others were about to leave. But for a few moments, they were all in the same room, and their reasons for being in here at that moment were exactly the same: They came to get something to eat."

"Problem is, even though that interest was shared, and they probably could have had a nice chat about the food for a while, the people who were fed were already done with this diner, and the people coming *in* were just getting started."

"Whoa, I think I get it! You mean we're all in varying stages of doing whatever the room we're in is all about. If you're fed, the diner is something you no longer need, but if you're hungry, it's incredibly important to you."

"There you go kiddo. For a little while you're all in the same room, and then you aren't. You could even extend it further to include the people who just sat down, the ones who've ordered, the ones who've been served, the ones who've eaten, the ones who've paid their bill, and the bunch we just saw, the ones exiting the room."

"Wow, that explains a lot, Sugar. People are at all sorts of different levels, busy experiencing what this particular room has to offer. They're all in the same room temporarily, but very few of them really notice how different their level is from the others around them."

"Right, Helen. They're all diners at the moment, all focused on the theme of this room, namely food, that's true. But at what level of the dining experience are they as diners?"

"I understand. Someone who just entered might stop and ask one of the people paying their bill how the food was, and that would be a common interest for a moment. But soon, the person who's leaving wants to leave. They obviously don't want to stay and chat about the food all the way through the other person's meal!"

I paused to think for a moment, then said, "So that's a big part of why so many relationships don't last? Somebody's just entering a room, and someone else has been there awhile but isn't quite done, and maybe there's somebody else who needs to move on right away. You could enter that room and not know the difference."

"Exactly," she said. "But it gets even more complicated because often the people in the room don't have any idea how much longer they're going to be there. Someone could be leaving the room tonight and not even know it."

"How in the world do you solve that problem, Sugar? It seems impossible."

Sugar smiled, "Not at all, honey. You just have to make sure that when you hook up with someone you take the time to see what they're about. And I mean *all* about. Nobody is about just one room."

"I'll give you an example. Let's say you meet someone at an art museum. Obviously you both like art or you wouldn't be there. But does that mean you'll like everything about that person? Hardly."

"You aren't going to spend your whole life in an art museum, but since lots of people consider themselves artists or lovers of the arts, they base their whole relationship on that one aspect, on that one room."

"It takes time and effort, of course, to find out about all the other rooms in a person's life, but it's essential. Remember, there are religious rooms, political rooms, sports rooms, bar rooms, family rooms...you name it."

"And just because a person is in a room you like, that doesn't make it an automatic match. After all, is every Democrat the same as every other Democrat, or every Methodist exactly the same as every other Methodist? Of course not."

"So take your time going in, whether it's dating, a new friendship, a relationship at work, or whatever. Make sure one of you isn't leaving the room while the other is just stepping in. Or that you don't view the contents of the room so radically differently that it will become a source of problems later."

Sugar looked at the wall clock and gave me a little pat on the shoulder. "Well, my break is over. I'll see ya honey," she said with a low, wheezy chuckle and quick smooth of her up-do before she turned to dash away.

"Sugar?" I called. "Thank you."

She stopped, smiled and waved away my thanks. "No big deal. Drop back in anytime. Banana cream pie is the dessert special on Wednesdays and in here, *every* day is Wednesday."

I got up then realized I didn't quite know what to do since I had no money with me. Sugar read my mind.

"Don't worry about the bill, kiddo. I'll put it on The Firemaker's tab," she said with a laugh. "Oh, and the next door? Just walk back out the way you came. You'll see. Bye-bye, honey."

Then, quick as could be, she was off serving coffee and counsel to another table.

I followed Sugar's directions, pushed against the revolving door, and stepped through it into The Garden. The Firemaker was there, quietly waiting.

CHAPTER 19

The Big Why

"Hello there, Helen! Did you have a nice time in the Diner?"

"Yes, I did and you know, this last door got me to thinking. When it comes to relationships, maybe it's better not to count on things working out a certain way. They never do, not the way I want, or the way anybody else I know wants them to either come to think of it."

"I take it you met Sugar."

I sure did. She was amazing. Showed me a thing or two with those little pots of cream. I'm not exactly sure what conclusion you hoped I'd draw from that experience. But before Sugar explained things, I was feeling pretty sorry for myself, going on and on about all of my crummy relationships.

"But like I was saying, even after all Sugar showed me, or maybe because of it, I'm more convinced than ever that it's better not to get overly invested in specific outcomes. It's just a setup for all kinds of problems. Maybe that's not a very enlightened attitude, but what else can you do? You can't control anyone. You can't make anyone *get it*."

"Yes, Helen, it's important to give your expectations lots of room to breathe. Very little is what it first seems, and the Universe is full of greater possibilities than you can imagine."

And yet it's also self-defeating to accept that things can go wrong and to focus on that until it becomes an expectation.

"They're two quite different perspectives, with the first leaving the door open to wonder and surprise, and the second building in problems because of past negative experiences."

"Hmmm. Yes, I see the difference. I'll really have to watch out for that in myself because I've sure done that second thing plenty of times."

Clearing my throat, I continued. "If I may, Firemaker, I have another question that's not directly related to what we've been talking about."

"Certainly, Helen. Ask away."

"Well, I understand about the search for this City of Joy place, but it doesn't explain how things work on a larger level, the level that explains what life is all about. And if I don't know what life is about, how can I work toward the outcome I want?"

I mean, even if I take the time in a relationship to make sure I'm not leaving a room as someone else is entering, and even if I allow my expectations lots of room to breathe, there's got to be more to the big picture. The Fourth Door certainly told me a lot about relationships, but that's only one piece of the puzzle.

"It seems to me that the way most of us live our lives is kind of insane. You know what I'm talking about, right? All the pain and the darkness. I can't believe it was meant to be this way. Tell me Firemaker, how did it all go so wrong?"

"The truth is, Helen, it hasn't all gone so wrong."

From far far away, well beyond this planet's atmosphere, even the largest cities on Earth are invisible to the naked eye. From there, the planet is perceived as a lovely, perfect blue ball and there's nothing dark or threatening about it.

"That may give you a sense of perspective. It's a good way for you to remember the enormity of the Cosmos."

Of course, human activity is important and especially so to humans. But in the grand scheme of things, it matters very little if human beings are behaving insanely for a while because, when you see the big picture, it's only a temporary aberration.

"Don't misunderstand; the madness you refer to can alter the progress of individual human souls, but it can't alter Cosmic Order."

No matter how it appears, everything is in balance even though at the level of your existence on the Earth plane it often seems quite the opposite.

"If that were not true, then a war, plane crash or earthquake might set the whole Universe spinning out of control. But, as you can see, that's *not* how it works. Far from it."

I thought for a moment then said, "I get that. I do, Firemaker. But if *you're* the one who's injured or killed in one of those situations, or it happens to someone you love, your *personal* universe *does* spin out of control. That's true for sure."

The Firemaker nodded. "Pain and trauma alter the progress of individual human souls, that's certain. But there is such a thing as Cosmic Law. If YOU could actually SEE the earth from a great distance, as the space traveler you dreamed of one day becoming when you were a little girl, you would see that even terrifying and horrible events occur within a greater order."

"Things that you find undesirable exist at the level of human life for many reasons, including the life of this planet. She has a Karmic existence of her own that is infinitely complex. And yet the spiral is one of life, not death, an ascending migration into which human thought is intrinsically woven."

Listening to her I felt like I was ascending, so thrilling were her words. And yet... something still troubled me and The Firemaker could read it all over my face.

"Perhaps this might help. What if you looked at the whole thing as a super-sized driving school with mandatory enrollment? But instead of an automobile, the learning is all about how to operate and steer the most intimate of all personal vehicles, your *Soul*."

"Inexperienced drivers crash into each other, or an event that's required by Cosmic Order intervenes in individual lives. That's when a collision happen."

I smiled but wasn't quite there yet.

The Firemaker nodded and continued. "Suppose you're watching a sweet yellow butterfly sip nectar from a flower. The sun is shining, the bees are buzzing and it's just a beautiful day in your life. Does that sound like a description of order?"

I nodded. "Absolutely!"

"But suddenly, a big blue jay swoops down and snatches the lovely little butterfly into its beak and gobbles it down right before your eyes. While it might be a shocking end to your idyllic scene of the previous moment, and fatal to the butterfly, does a bird eating a butterfly seem out of order? Does it seem as if suddenly everything in life has gone so wrong?"

"Well, no. That's just the nature of things. Birds eat butterflies, whether I like it or not."

"Correct, Helen. People kill other people, planes crash, and powerful hurricanes destroy lives and property, and on and on, whether humans like it or not. Because at this time in the evolution of the earth and its creatures..."

"That's just the nature of things, right?" I said.

"Yes. But that's not really what you're talking about. You're talking about how those kinds of things *feel* to you."

"Yes, that's it. I don't like it. I don't even like it that birds eat butterflies."

"I understand. But do you think that these things will be changing any time soon? All the wars, the damage to the planet and natural disasters and butterfly-eating birds?"

I didn't have to think long about that one. "No, I'm afraid not."

"Very well. Then right now, and I'm only talking about your existence at this level at this time, your task is not to understand all there is to understand about why Cosmic Order looks the way it does on the planet upon which you live."

"Your task is to understand that what upsets you does so because part of you want things to be different, and part of you knows that an enormous amount of it need not be."

"But it is your longing for things to be different that motivates you...to free yourself of those aspects of your own being that in truth, do not belong to you. This is why you're on this journey."

Something inside of me softened a little and I could feel myself begin to unwind.

"So," The Firemaker continued, "there's *not* something inherently wrong in the cosmos. If we modify what the Buddha said—that 'Life is suffering'—to 'Life *includes* suffering', this seeming broken system becomes just a little easier to live with."

You wish that life didn't include suffering, Helen. I understand. I do, too. But on this plane at this time, it does."

"Yes, Firemaker, but natural disasters and accidents are one thing. Wars and murder and all of that kind of mayhem are human creations and, well, it's just not right."

The Firemaker nodded. "Helen, one of the reasons things are the way they are on Earth, both good and bad in your perception, is because people create out of what they believe, and that can be anything to anyone at anytime."

"There is a difference between natural order and malevolent personal will. We touched on this some time back. Do you remember?"

"I do."

"Good. Then this would be an excellent time to round that out. Human beings are free to make their own choices about how they want to live, even if it's destructive to other human beings. And here's where knowledge of the law of belief plus action comes into play."

"If you don't believe it can be done, you're right. But on the other hand, if you think something's difficult but you still believe that you can do it, and you take action based upon that belief, many times it unfolds exactly the way you want it to."

"That's what happened back at the Beehive when you believed so completely that you wanted out, and then found your way out, with a little help from me."

"But what about when I exercise my personal will and things go exactly the opposite of what I want?"

"That would be a situation where you've been trumped by cosmic order. Life's a partnership between personal will and cosmic order, a compromise between what you want and what must be in order to maintain balance in the Universe."

Just because you choose a course and set out on it doesn't mean that you'll always arrive at the exact destination you picked. Sometimes you will and sometimes you won't.

"If there are other circumstances you didn't have knowledge of when you made your choice, other events that must occur to keep things in universal balance, then your will cannot counter that."

"But that doesn't mean it won't triumph in many, or even most situations. It will, and being alive implies that you must do something with your life force."

And yes, as you said, some people will use theirs to choose a path of destruction, and the human-made horrors of life ensue.

If you continue your journey through the seven doors, you will learn more about people making destructive choices and about how these choices can feed darkness and take root within many systems of the world.

"That learning, and the other teachings associated with it, will unlock some of the mysteries that have troubled your heart for so long. But there's much work to be done before you reach that point."

I thought about what The Firemaker said for a minute. She was right. I wasn't ready. There was more to do, and knowing that gave me hope and the energy to continue.

CHAPTER 20

Belief Is A Personal Journey

"Firemaker? Can I ask you something? Every religion I'm aware of says the world is god-designed and that our lives are governed by a system of perfect order, like the cosmic order you spoke about earlier. Taking into consideration the differences, at least according to what I've been able to glean, they all seem to indicate that eventually, if we're good, we'll end up in some version of the City of Joy. But if we're bad, well, it's pretty much the Terrible Desert for all eternity."

"So in practice, and I'm no expert, no one really knows how things work or how to get to the City of Joy for sure. How then can any of us ever hope to grow past our human created suffering if we don't know what we're doing or why we're doing it? I figure the fact that I'm still struggling shows how much growing I still have to do. But here it is anyway – what I really need is an answer to the BIG WHY in the Sky."

The Firemaker smiled and spoke even more softly. "Your questions, Helen, come from the very center of who you are. They are deeply yours, and also the agony of All souls in All Time."

"You are asking me, I think, about human-kind's systems for addressing questions that do not have obvious answers unless one believes in invisible powers, such as a Supreme Being who cannot be seen or touched."

I nodded in agreement.

"Remember, since belief plus action is how we create, and since creation is what you're here to do, your personal will allows you to believe as you want, and you may choose good or ill to believe in and act upon. But once you've made your choice and taken action on it, your whole world changes a little, or sometimes a lot, to fit your choice."

That doesn't mean you can choose to have the Sun flicker out and it will happen. As I said, there's such a thing as cosmic order, and no one being can simply cancel that out with belief.

"But, you can choose what you will believe in and dedicate yourself to it and much of what you're after will come to you."

"So, your choice to believe in a Supreme Being or not is entirely yours, though people have argued for many ages as to whether such a being exists. It's not my place to settle that debate. The discovery of belief is a personal journey, a part of your evolution, and a gift of your freedom and the path of your individual vehicle, your soul."

What I can tell you, though, is that the Arc Of Life begins before birth and continues after death. From this point you cannot see the whole of your soul's path, but since you're here, on this marvelous planet, at this moment in it's existence and yours, you must do something.

"Yes, you can choose to do nothing. But then what you're really doing is allowing your body's life force to ebb. And because of the nature of things, soon your earthly life will be gone and you won't be able to get it back. You only have so much time in this physical body."

"I think I understand, Firemaker. I'm here and even though I don't know why I'm here, practically nobody else does either, so I might as well just stop worrying about knowing the unknowable and get on with life, right?"

"Right. And?"

"And when I reach the appropriate level, more will be revealed. So, whether I decide to claim a BIG WHY belief system or participate as I feel to, I'm still functioning within cosmic order and the laws of life. I'm choosing what to believe in and then acting upon that belief, right?"

The Firemaker nodded. "Yes. And the rest of it, 'the big WHY in the Sky,' as you put it, will come when you're ready, when you need to know in order to keep progressing, instead of just wanting to know."

"But that's enough about that for now because it's time for you to go through the next door. There's still much for you to learn."

Without another word, The Firemaker pointed to the Fifth Door. A picture of a small loaf of bread was painted on its tile. I took a deep breath, sighed just a little, and opened the door.

CHAPTER 21

The Fifth Door

It was snowing. I quickly buttoned the toggle clasp at the neck of my blue windbreaker and began to walk. After a while I came upon a narrow, dimly lit street that eventually lead to a cobblestoned quarter right out of a Charles Dickens' novel. Pulling the cord at the hem of my windbreaker tighter, I shoved my hands into the pockets and kept walking, drawn by the light of a distant lamp and the delicious aroma of freshly baked bread.

I had found the bakery. Like a hummingbird readying to dive a Christmas cactus, I hovered in the doorway, drawing the cloud of yeasted sugar deep into my lungs. Despite my embarrassing display of excess in the diner, I try to stay away from treats. I really do. But unfortunately, the appetite for this sort of thing is hardwired into my DNA.

If you're the sort of person who loves baked goods, this place was heaven by the mouthful. Chocolate delights and jammy cakes, sticky buns and cheesy strudel, fritters and sweet breads, blueberry tartlets and cherry scones by the dozens flew from an enormous oven into pink boxes swiftly tied up with bows made of string.

Whatever you wanted, whatever you imagined, this bakery delivered. Despite the hour, despite the neighborhood, it was a bustling place and precious as a Tiffany box. Walls and ceiling painted the same hue – a cheerful shade of blue that made everything feel special and fine.

In her tall white hat and apron, the baker stood behind the counter, which was curiously low, briskly directing a dozen or more nimble helpers. To her right, near the front of the bakery, a staircase lead to another counter with another baker, also busily directing helpers. I didn't notice when I first walked in, but now I could plainly see that the upstairs customers waited with more ease, absent the awkwardly positioned counter.

Once they'd placed their orders, the customers settled down a bit, naturally. But only a few, I noticed, climbed up the staircase to the second floor. Though it seemed the obvious better choice, most remained on the crowded ground floor.

Strangely, at least I thought so; the bakers didn't pay much attention to the customers. There was no chit chat, no discussion, just a swift checking of the order and then off to helpers who quickly gathered the ingredients, mixed, and then popped batter and dough into the huge oven.

Apparently free to choose between the two counters, the customers placed their orders and then moved aside to enter a glassed-in room – there was one on each floor – to watch and wait in comfort as it was prepared.

The people upstairs appeared content to read or even leave the shop and let the baker do her work, happy to pick up their order when it was ready.

But on the ground floor, the majority who'd put in their orders kept going back to the counter – even after the helpers had begun mixing, which only forced them to stop and start over.

"More nuts," shouted one man. "Less yeast," said another before dashing back into the waiting room. Round and round the helpers went, trying to keep up with customer demands. But the baker remained entirely neutral. Nothing seemed to rattle her.

By now I was *really* hungry. Everything looked *soooo* good. Suddenly the rush had passed and there was no one at the lower counter. Stooping a bit, I seized the opportunity and gave my order to the baker.

"Raisin bread, please," I said and went into the waiting room.

It's a funny thing about waiting for what you want. It was obvious to me that the people at the upper counter were content to wait. But those at the lower counter, the ones who kept changing their orders, well, they didn't settle down for long. And neither did I.

Considering all I'd been through behind the other doors, you'd think I'd have known better than to do what I did next, but – nope.

With so much restlessness and milling about, I found it impossible to wait patiently after I gave my order to the baker.

"Will I get what I ordered or is this place some kind of rip off?" one woman grumbled.

"How do I know this baker is any good? She's not very friendly!" said another.

When the woman next to me ran in and changed her order to banana bread, I was sunk.

"Mmmm. Banana bread! Why didn't I order Banana Bread? That would have been a much better choice, sweeter, moister, all around tastier."

"It's okay to change your order, isn't it? Everyone down here is doing it and besides, I should be able to change my mind if I want to, shouldn't I?"

That was it. Once I went down that path I couldn't stop myself. Under the ceiling fan I ducked, running back to the lower counter to call out a new order.

"I've changed my mind!" I shouted. "I want banana bread!"

Finally content, I went back into the waiting room and tried to settle down. But it was not to be. A woman sitting next to me got up, ran back in and changed her order to whole wheat.

"Whole wheat! That's what I want! It's so much healthier. Plus the fiber! I think I'll make mine whole wheat, too. Heck, how about *organic* while I'm at it?"

And so I changed my order again.

And again.

And again.

By the time I was done, I must have changed my order fifteen times. I'm sure you can guess what happened. Flat as a pancake and burnt to a crisp, it was loaded with chunks of something unidentifiable—definitely *not* raisins—and a blackened banana peel sticking out of the top.

I was disgusted with myself. But my time in the Land Behind the Doors had taught me a thing or two: when in doubt, go out the way you came in. And if that fails, look for the nearest alternative exit. It can usually be found right under your nose. I ditched the loathsome loaf and left the Bakery by the back door.

CHAPTER 22

All One

As usual, The Firemaker was waiting for me on the Little Bridge.

"A little unpalatable, Helen?"

"Yeah, my order wasn't exactly the treat I'd hoped for."

"No, it didn't look particularly tasty. But you've learned something important that you'll never forget. The learning was the point, not the treat, because the experiences of the Fifth Door were meant to teach you about the Greater and Lesser Selves."

"Greater and Lesser Selves?"

"Yes, she nodded. "The Lesser Self, as I think you're beginning to see, is a place where much of humanity spends a major part of their lifetime. Please understand me, there's no judgment in my words. Everyone has a Lesser Self. It's just how people are made up."

"But you said there was a Greater Self, too. You mean there's another Self in me somewhere?"

"Not literally. Ultimately everything about you is part of the same self. But it will be far easier to understand this lesson if you temporarily think of the Greater and Lesser Selves as being separate."

"You see The Greater Self, what some call the Infinite Self, is the intuition-guided, super-conscious self and the Lesser Self is part of the same being, but functions at a much different, denser level. It is dependent and uncertain by nature, demanding what it needs by necessity."

"It isn't a bad thing. Not at all. Infants exist in this state because they cannot care for themselves. One of the Lesser Self's purposes is to make sure the child's caregivers know when it wants or needs things."

"But the Greater Self is always present, existing at a much finer, quieter, more secure state than the Lesser Self. Present from the moment of birth, its nature is so patient and exquisitely subtle that it can take much guidance and dedicated work to realize it even exists."

"And it takes even more guidance and dedicated work to let the Greater Self take charge of one's wellbeing."

"You might think of the Lesser Self as a seed or tiny sprout, something in the process of becoming whatever its potential says it can be. That is the essence of the Greater Self. Even the giant redwood was once just a tiny, fragile seed—far removed from the potential of what it would one day become."

"But, Firemaker, what keeps us from shooting up into our Greater Selves and being done with this slow-growing Lesser Self nonsense? I'm fed up with her! Just when I think I've got it, she shows up and gets me in trouble."

"I understand, Helen. You're right in the middle of it all now. Perhaps this will help you. In Cosmic terms, human beings are the same, in essence, as a giant redwood. It takes a long time to grow into a fully integrated life form."

"And there's one more evolutionary step above that, the *Unified Spirit*, but I'll come back to that in a bit. For now, let's think back to the Bakery so you'll fully understand this lesson."

"The part of the mind that helps the Greater and the lesser Selves attain what they desire is the subconscious mind—in this situation, represented by the Baker behind the counter."

The subconscious mind is the Facilitator, working on behalf of both states of being, the Greater and the Lesser Selves. It's neutral, without a will of its own.

"It doesn't judge or understand humor, sarcasm or irony. It takes every demand—every order—that comes over the counter literally and immediately acts on it."

"Of course! Now I get why there were two levels and two counters in the Bakery!"

"The bottom level represents the Lower Self. Everything was lower including the counter, the cakes, and the mirror."

"So the people at that level, including me, were operating from our Lower Selves and, well, pretty much acting like impatient children."

"The upper level represents the Greater Self. The counter was at a functional height and the people who placed their orders were mature, courteous and patient. Clearly they were operating from their Greater Selves. I get it."

"Yes, Helen. Once the Baker – the subconscious mind – has the order from either of the two Selves, it must attempt to fill it."

"But the order can only be filled if the demand is strong enough and held in consciousness *as placed* long enough for the order to be completely 'baked,' so to speak."

"When that happens, then the thing desired – or strongly feared for that matter – is focused into being. Eventually it comes out of the Baker's oven and into one's reality."

"And that's why my order came out so messed up and lousy. I kept changing the ingredients. And since the Baker doesn't argue, she just kept redoing it as ordered until I'd made a complete mess of it, right?"

"Exactly. I realize that you've read or heard about this truth in many venues and thought it little more than nonsense or wishful thinking. But even though *your* experiences have not delivered this truth to you, that doesn't keep it from being true."

"Without understanding this, life appears to be little more than random happening after random happening and you a victim of its whims. But it's not so."

"You're giving the Baker orders all the time, whether you know it or not. It's how individual human beings create things. There's no other way to do it."

"I think I understand, Firemaker. The sole job of the subconscious mind, the Baker, is to facilitate. Its job is to get the order out, not be a wishes-and-desires cop. It does whatever it can to assist...how do I put it?..in the creation of what the Greater or the Lesser Self are focused on, right?"

"That's right. The Baker doesn't invent or edit the recipes. She simply reads them and acts upon them exactly as the individual customer hands them to her. She's neutral. Completely neutral."

"You see, most people think the way they are right now, inhabiting the lesser, more earth-bound regions of the Self, is all there is to reality, or as you'd say, 'The System.' And for you to understand this System, it's important for you to grasp the nature of the Lesser Self."

"It might be helpful to think of the Lesser Self as an actual baby, and the only thing baby knows is what it wants. You could say *wanting* is its job. It constantly desires and needs, is limited and demanding, and has little or no comprehension of where it's going."

"Because it knows nothing other than itself, it believes that itself, as it is today, is all there is or can ever be. It's the essence of all that's still in need of assistance and guidance in human beings."

"Just like a baby, the Lesser Self has the potential to grow, but unlike a baby, emotional and psychological growth don't come automatically, or even on any particular schedule. In fact, the growth of the Lesser Self has little to do with physical age. When you encounter someone living exclusively in the Lesser Self, he or she could be nine months or ninety years old."

"The Firemaker paused. "If I'm going too fast, Helen, please let me know."

"It's a lot to take in all at once, yes, but I'm with you all the way, Firemaker. Go on, please."

"Very well. As you've seen, the subconscious – the Facilitator or Baker – is designed to accomplish only specific tasks. It also acts as a bridge between the Lesser and the Greater Selves. When the Lesser Self cries out wanting something, it's actually giving an order to the Baker to figure out how to obtain what it wants."

"Many people, and you're one of them, know bits and pieces of information about the Lesser Self. But what most don't know, what you haven't known, is that the Greater Self will always try to protect you, always try to elevate your existence, while the Lesser Self is barely even aware that something greater could exist."

"The Greater Self is always with you, Helen, and it cares for you unconditionally, without judgment, hurry or frustration. It can see all the possibilities for you and is available to guide you toward becoming your highest and best self."

"That means it can't intervene in your life unless you're open to its guidance. You see, for it to step in without your permission, except during the extreme danger of a life-threatening crisis, isn't possible because that would diminish your choices and negate your personal will."

"When one is at the earlier levels of growth, the Greater Self is there, mostly just observing until a person is able, or simply ready to listen."

"Without an open invitation from you, it can't intervene in daily life except to nudge you quietly with a giant burst of warning intuition in a crisis. You must grow until you're aware of the Greater Self and then invite it to take over. Rest assured, it knows infinitely more than the Lesser Self."

"You've been preparing to invite your Greater Self in for a long time, Helen. Although you haven't been aware of it, it's always been available to you, helping in ways that don't interfere with your personal will. When you've passed through seven doors, you'll know what it means to live life through the choices of the Greater Self."

"Helen, I promised you that I would explain what can happen when the Lesser and Greater Selves unite with the subconscious."

"As I said, now and then, although not often on the Earth plane, both selves and the subconscious evolve and become fully integrated and function as one being – a *Unified Spirit*."

"I believe you know of some who have achieved this state?"

"Yes," I said, thinking of some of the sacred names familiar to all.

The Firemaker nodded. "And there are others, too, many whose names will never be known."

"Once a human being has managed to transform the heavy baggage of the Lesser Self into the power to release all control of his or her life to the Greater Self, he or she can then fully unite with the subconscious."

"At that point another transformation takes place. Again, it's very rare on the Earth plane, but once it happens, that person becomes a Unified Spirit."

"For a Unified Spirit, there's no longer anything left to slow down its evolution. It doesn't think; it automatically *knows* what's desirable for itself and others, and what is not."

"Through many fits and starts, through much trial and error, the Unified Spirit has acquired the tools it needed to become whole."

"Remember, all Unified Spirits once lived ordinary human lives, just like you. Their paths and times in history may have been different, but each achieved the transition from a fragmented state of being to a unified state of being."

"Many people know of the famous ones, but you can also encounter a person at any station in life who could be one, even though the person's appearance gives no hint of it. You can't tell from the outer trappings, only by the actions and totality of the life lived."

"That's why Unified Spirits are rarely recognized during their lifetime for what they truly are. It takes people looking back on the total life to finally see who and what they were."

"So, are you saying that this unification of the Selves and the Baker—the subconscious—is what we're here to do? Is that the true purpose of life?"

"There is more, Helen, but yes. This is a major part of it. And you are also here to assist other beings in the same quest. The task of living a human life could be conceived of as learning to understand your true and complete nature, your wholeness, and then directing it toward what you want to create from that knowing. Even at the lower levels, your thoughts have the power to help you bring forth what *you* want, for good or ill."

"But when you achieve awareness and control of the Lesser Self, letting the Greater Self guide you intuitively, and allowing the subconscious mind to do its job, you become truly free to create an existence of inner peace and harmony that will lead to becoming a Unified Spirit one day."

"When you were a little girl, your grandmother gave you a special doll. Do you remember?"

"I do! She was unlike any other in my dollhouse. Her belly was yellow and she wore a garland of flowers around her head," I said, making a sweeping gesture to demonstrate the garland. "Inside of her there was a smaller doll. And inside that doll, another, even smaller."

The Firemaker nodded and smiled. "One doll made of many."

I smiled, too, remembering how I would open and close her, one becoming many, many becoming one. I was beginning to understand.

"Don't be overly concerned with the details of what I've told you, Helen," The Firemaker said. "Simply recall her. She will help you, with these four simple statements, sense how this works."

"The innermost doll, your Lesser Self, is the *Desiring Self*, a kind of infant consciousness."

"The middle doll, your *Facilitator* or subconscious mind— the one we're calling the Baker—is the active agent who brings together and mixes the ingredients of your desires."

"The mother or parent doll, your Greater Self, is the *Knowing Self* that always tries to lift you above the Lesser Self."

"Once those three entities are in complete unison, the *Unified Spirit* is realized."

I nodded. "It's clearer now, at least most of it."

"That's good, Helen. Very good. This is an important lesson and it will give you a personal way to view something that's not so personal. It's a lot to absorb, I know... Do you think you can take in a little more?"

CHAPTER 23

The Cave

"Yes, Firemaker, please go on. I can see that without knowing how we evolve as spiritual beings, just passing through the doors won't get me where I want to be."

"Even after all I've learned in the Land Behind the Doors, look at what silly choices I made at the Bakery."

"Don't be harsh with yourself, Helen. That's excellent insight, about your own growth. Instead of judging the other people at the Bakery, notice that you chose to be introspective about your own actions. That's an enormous change in your point of view from the first few doors. Remember that *you* also deserve not to be judged. It's not enough to know this about others. It must also flow from you to you."

"I want to remind you that, while it's helpful to think of the Lesser Self, the Greater Self and the Facilitator as three separate entities—three separate dolls—there is no actual separation. They are one, and within the one are *many* facets, many aspects that make up the wholeness of a being. Life is dynamic, and of a continuum. Your existence, Helen Brower, is no different."

"You have this understanding now. It's yours, which means we can continue a little further into even more understanding. How does that sound?"

"Yes, let's keep going!"

"All right then. Can you imagine a cave? A deep one?"

I could. "Yes, Firemaker, I am imagining it right now."

The Firemaker smiled and continued. "This cave gets narrower and narrower at the back until the space is so small a person standing up can touch both sides and the roof easily. Imagine that, from there, that person can see a tiny point of light far, far away at the opening. The cave slopes upward toward that light at the opening, making climbing all the way up and out extremely challenging.

"Next, think of the Lesser Self as existing at the narrow back of the cave down where there isn't much light and almost no space."

"Obviously, if we move up the cave toward the open end, the further we walk, the more space and light there is. That forward, outward motion is the Self, expanding."

"When it's way down at the bottom, there's little room to move, not much to light the way, and it's very easy to imagine that this is all there is or ever could be."

"But by constantly looking to the Light and moving toward it, the Self expands, sees more possibilities for growth and, over time, reaches the opening of the cave where there are no walls, only space and light."

"During this process, everyone climbs up, then slips back down, many, many times. You may not go all the way back to the bottom when you slip, what the people in the Auditorium would call 'bottoming out,' but you *will* slip, then rise, slip, then rise."

"Eventually, the number of your rises will far outweigh your slips downward, and you *will* exit the cave once and for all."

"When that point is reached, a being has become a Unified Spirit and there are no further limits or lack of opportunity for that being. Anything is possible, everything lies open and before you at that place."

"Every single being is heading there eventually. It may not happen within the confines of the limited existence of one Earthly personality, but you are not your personality. When there is no longer a Helen Brower on Earth, there will still be a *you*, growing, expanding, and reaching into the Light forever. Do you see?" she asked.

By now I had tears in my eyes; the beauty of what she was giving to me was so overwhelming. "Oh yes, Firemaker, I do see. And it's a tremendous relief! You're telling me that slipping and going backward isn't the end of the world. And, even more importantly, what we call 'death' is – well, not the end of my evolution."

"Wonderful! Yes, Helen. I'm glad you understand. You are infinite. And you will get there."

"This has been a lot to take in, I know, so let's leave it for now. Because, if you're ready, I believe it's time for you to move on to the Sixth Door."

"But I still have many questions, Firemaker."

"And eventually they'll all be answered, but the next door awaits... unless you need a rest or No, no, I'm ready. Here I go!"

The Firemaker pointed to the door in front of me with a little blue sailboat painted on its tile and I moved toward it.

CHAPTER 24

The Sixth Door

As I stepped through the Sixth Door I knew where I was and it felt like coming home. This was the inlet on the Little Dreamy I'd seen that first day I met Peri. The little blue sailboat was still tethered to the dock, the water gently lapping against her sides.

So sweet and perfectly sized for me, I had to peek inside. On the bottom of her hull, neatly stacked atop a metal case no bigger than a hatbox, a brass compass the size of my fist squarely anchored a piece of paper folded into a small square.

I couldn't resist a closer look, so I boarded her and picked up the compass and paper underneath. It was a map charting the location of a group of islands in a delta not far from the inlet. And inside the metal case there were enough rations for a day trip – sandwich, thermos of water, crackers, dried fruit and nuts.

The map charted the location of six small rivers and pictured large the Little Dreamy emptying out into a delta. Beyond, where her fresh water joined with the sea, was a group of islands likely not too far away. If one of these islands was my destination, I crossed my fingers for it to be a quick trip there and back.

After reviewing the map, I spotted a small green arrow and felt suddenly compelled to go to where it pointed. You should know that back then, not only was I no sailor, I'd never even *been* sailing. What's more, when it comes to directions, I don't know east from up. And, just as important, water and I never had a complete reconciliation, not after that time I got lost in the heart of the undertow when I was a little girl.

I was about seven, I think, and the family was spending a rare week of vacation at the beach. I wasn't familiar with ocean swimming and somehow I managed to find the riptide right off the bat.

Fortunately, before I ran out of kicking and flapping power, a lifeguard appeared. He knew how to take me parallel to the shore rather than swim head on against the riptide, and that saved me. But for that ninety-second eternity before he got to me, when I couldn't breathe or even see the shoreline, the seven-year old me was sure I wouldn't make it out of there.

I didn't completely quit the water after that. I still swam a little if I thought it wasn't too deep, but I never went into it again with the same fearless confidence I'd had before.

That meant that meeting the challenge of the Sixth Door, sailing out all by myself, was going to require a real leap of faith.

I looked at the map, then at the compass, then at the map again. These should have been enough, but since I had no idea how to sail, I was at a loss and about to get out of the boat and look for help when I saw a small bundle of rope coiled near the tiller with a note pinned on the top.

"Pull Me," it read, which I did, instantly setting off a series of events. The boom slid over my head and the sail fluttered loudly, then filled with a gust of wind as the little boat leaned over and began to glide away from the shore.

At first I was shaky about being on the water all alone, but finally I managed to relax a little, then, when things went well, a little more, and then, when nothing bad happened, a whole lot more. I sailed easily for an hour or two. The boat seemed to know what it was doing, and that was a good thing, since *I* certainly didn't.

Then, unexpectedly, the breeze that had so softly carried me this far quickened, and I soon found myself battling angry winds and fierce currents. I was in big trouble.

Blinking back the tears, my heart pounding, I bore down on the rudder trying to keep the boat on course, but she had a mind of her own and sailed into the storm, riding high atop the waves, and then plummeting wildly into the troughs.

The boat struggled desperately to climb a wall of water that only moments ago had been safe sky, and we were pitched again atop the waves, bow pointed toward the heavens.

This went on for what seemed like hours. Frantically trying not to be thrown overboard or have my head cracked open by the boom, I tied myself to the boat with a rope and began bailing water as fast as it poured in.

I managed to save myself from those fates, but my efforts to take control of the situation were useless as my hands blistered and my face went numb from the driving rain. I was in the fight of my life, terrified as the wind and seething river spat the little boat back and forth at their mercy.

Until now in the Land Behind the Doors, when I was afraid or couldn't imagine a way out, I'd cry out for The Firemaker. But this time was different. While my Lesser Self wailed inside, my Greater Self stayed in charge and I chose not to collapse within and stick it out on my own, fueled by a surge of inner resolve that gave me the strength to carry on through those awful hours.

After a seemingly endless night of struggle, morning finally came, and with it, the end of the storm. It was a great relief — for about as long as it took me to catch my breath.

Soon, I realized that my troubles were *not* over. I was past the delta and out to sea. Land just a faint outline on the horizon, I was adrift with no wind or current to take me back to shore.

Where only a short time ago there'd been too much wind, now there was too little. No breeze, no movement, no end in sight. It was as if a drought had come and turned my world into a place of stillness and silence so impenetrable, I could do little more than just *be*. By noon the heat and glare were overwhelming with my windbreaker the only shelter.

That bit of shade was critical to my survival, but it didn't help maintain the resolve that had gotten me through the storm. That was slipping away with the lowering of the sun.

The thought of another night adrift was almost unbearable and I came to a point of despair. Only flashes of courage from my Greater Self kept me from losing hope completely, but there were moments when I had almost none, when my thoughts were as bleak and dark as the night that closed in around me.

Restless and full of doubt, why had I done this to myself? Why had I put myself in harm's way? I could be safe, on dry land, curled snug on the green sofa.

But even as I lamented my predicament, I knew that my decision to follow The Firemaker had not been wrong. Had I not chosen to go on this journey, my restlessness, which was never far away, would've taken hold again, driving me from the sanctuary I found in Peri's garden.

Finally the sun reappeared and though I waited all that day, still there was no wind. Feeling lost and alone, I cautiously rationed my food and the last drops of water from the thermos.

Then, at last, just as the sun went down again, a slight breeze came up and softly filled the sails, gently washing the boat toward a small island.

Off the shore where the water was shallow I put on my windbreaker, gathered the map, compass, and what was left of the provisions, hopped out and carefully dragged the boat onto the beach, grateful to be on dry land.

The moon had risen, and the evening was swiftly growing cool. In my damp clothes, I began to tremble from the cold.

I made my way up a small rise to a grove of trees growing near the water's edge and found shelter under their dark branches. Exhausted and thirsty, the night breeze rustling through the leaves soothed me, and I fell into a deep sleep.

CHAPTER 25

Smashing The Pearl

I don't know what time it was when I awoke, maybe 3:00 in the morning? Through weary half-closed eyes, I noticed something shimmering in the dark not more than five yards away.

I got up, walked over, reached down slowly and cautiously touched it. The size and shape of a soccer ball, it was hard, opalescent and warm to the touch. I felt compelled to pick it up, just like I'd felt compelled to follow the green arrow.

Much heavier than I expected, a wave of pain surged through my body, causing me to loose my balance.

Stumbling backwards, I flung it from me to be rid of the pain. It fell hard against a boulder, shattering into a heap of gritty white powder.

Not knowing if I'd done a good thing or a bad thing, I dropped to my knees and saw something lying amidst the rubble that made my eyes fill with tears. It was small, beautiful and bright beyond belief. I knew instantly what it was.

Placing it over my heart I was overcome with emotion. The feeling of seeing your best and dearest friend after years and years of separation poured through every ounce of my being. I was complete, whole, fulfilled.

As the stone rested on my breast, something miraculous began to happen. It was as if a vault in my mind, long locked and sealed, began to swing open. In came the light and the forgotten memory of a little girl searching for a piece of the sun. It was pure joy, and I knew that what I was experiencing was true.

I had finally found my Sunstone!

The wind began to swirl and dart, reminding me of my chill and that there were still hours to go before morning. Sunstone in hand, I began to search for tinder and kindling to make a fire. The Sunstone lit my way and soon I found dry twigs and branches downed by the storm.

I didn't have matches, but instinct told me that, by striking the edge of the Sunstone against something solid like a sharp rock, it would make sparks but not be harmed.

At first the twigs wouldn't catch, but then I remembered the law and I believed that I could make a fire and I took action to support that belief. It wasn't easy, but I kept at it, and on the seventh or eighth try, I made a small fire.

I was pleased with myself, I must say, and suddenly everything was just so, well, *clear*.

It was as if I'd never seen fire before. Looking back, it seems elementary now. But in a way that was true – I'd never really *seen* fire before, at least not like I was seeing it right then.

I thought back to that first day on the bus when I'd met Virgie and that voice in my head asked, "What other miracles are you ignoring in your life, Helen?"

I marveled at how the darkness receded as the flames grew. With each new log, the night shrank, and I could see ever more vividly where I was.

It seems almost silly when I say this because it's so obvious, but as I said, I'd never paid attention to fire before. It brings heat and light and moves back the darkness, but before that night I'd always taken the elements of fire as one lumped-together event. I hadn't appreciated what actually happens during each distinct step of making one.

The fire continued to grow, and the bigger it got, the smaller became my fears until that old familiar cold place in the center of my chest squeezed tight one last time and burst into nothingness, destroyed by the heat of the flames and my determination to complete my journey through the doors.

I'd had to go through six of the Seven Doors, and I had to face my fear of water to achieve this feeling, but so many things were visible now that hadn't been before. Everything was as clear to me as the bright red, orange and yellow flames dancing in front of my eyes.

Until this moment I'd been tired and sad, with a heart full of abandoned dreams. I'd forgotten who I was, deep down in the center of me. My truth had become buried under layers of ill-formed beliefs about who I was and who I was not. Never more than lies cast long ago, they'd festered into nothing less than self-prophecy and self-perpetuated distortions.

The realization was overwhelming to me. I felt the way an animal must when it's been caught in a snare yet somehow manages to free itself. I threw back my head into the night, flung my arms toward the stars and cried out, "I've smashed the Pearl! No more darkness!!!"

The feeling of relief was enormous, so complete and new that I hadn't noticed the color of the sky. The night had ended.

My gaze fell on the map, and I was surprised to see something I hadn't been aware of until now. I picked it up and looked more closely. 'In addition to the large green arrow, there was another icon – a little yellow star marking Star Island downstream from the direction I'd fought so hard to go. Instinctively, I knew this was where I was now.

At that moment, a breathtaking insight came to me. Struggling to go where I thought I *should*, I'd fought against the elements as I'd always fought against everything that was easy and good and right *for me*.

All my life I'd insisted on sailing *upstream*, not knowing that I could never, ever find my happiness that way. I'd sought it anywhere but on the current that ran naturally in the other direction — the direction of my Downstream Dream of Wholeness.

I wanted to know more of this island, so I began to walk inland. A gentle wind blew off the river and calmed whatever restlessness remained in my heart. The deep silence gave me steadiness, and the open space and sweet air filled my soul with stillness.

When I was desperately thirsty, I came across a little freshwater stream, a gift from The Firemaker, I'm sure. I drank my fill, topped off my thermos and ate the last of the stale sandwich from my rations. It was hard and chewy, but I was so hungry it was ambrosia to me.

My newfound peace of mind filled me with a delicate solace that enabled me to walk for hours without fatigue or discomfort. This island of harmony was a place I instinctively knew was as much a part of me as the color of my eyes and the shape of my hands.

I was expanding quickly inside, becoming more aware of my truest desires, needs and wants, seeing that they resided in my Downstream Dream and nowhere else. To find them, I had to go in the direction of the flow, sometimes riding it out if it got rough, but relaxing and trusting rather than pushing against it.

The Downstream Dream lived inside me, had always been there, always available for me to care for and nurture into my life. It was embedded in every cell of my being, and in everything I loved. Soft and accommodating, it whispered like the tone of a distant bell, a sound that lingered but did not deafen the voice of my personal will.

Surely I could have reached some mediocre upstream destination. With perseverance, I probably could have made it to some version of the City of Stability and been afraid to leave, calling it good enough. I'd spent my whole life up to that point doing some version of exactly that. Lots of people do. But now I knew that, even if I'd achieved that objective, I would have never have been at peace. Only by following my Downstream Dream could I find what I truly needed, revealed to me through the guidance of my heart.

Now I knew better than to be suspicious of what came to me on gentle currents. Now I knew better than to think that if something came easily, it had no value.

It was true, if you believe you can't do something you're likely not going to take the necessary steps to create what burns in you to bring it forth. Yes, we are here to create, and belief plus action is how we do it. It is a law of life. I understood that now. And there was something else, too.

My whole life I'd been waiting for something outside me to fill my inner emptiness. Now, I knew everything I could ever want or need was inside me, inside the Downstream Dream of Wholeness that is the very core of who I am.

Though I'd nearly lost the ability to know this, it was there still, a river of goodness that flowed beneath the sorrow that covered its brightness, *my* brightness.

The Sunstone was mine. It had been with me all this time, shrouded inside the Pearl. To find it, I had to go through that darkest of dark nights.

I had to look at myself straight on and claim that I was done selling myself short and that I would create my life from the gifts of my downstream dream. I would put down what was not true and fill my arms with the luminous light surging through every lonely and painful atom of my being. I would hold this new beauty fast, and from now on, to chart my course; I would live in the truth of what I knew and look to the future and my downstream dreams to find my way.

CHAPTER 26

New Eyes

As I explored the island, I was aware that eventually The Firemaker or the next door would appear. Sure enough, just when I felt I'd been there long enough, I turned a corner in a small valley and came upon a signpost shaped like a pointing hand:

THIS WAY TO THE GARDEN

A few yards more and I saw The Firemaker. She was waiting for me at the Little Bridge and I was thrilled to see her.

"Hello, Helen!" she said.

"Firemaker – hello! I'm soooo glad to see you again! The island was just incredible. This whole journey is incredible!"

"So, you've gotten around to enjoying yourself, I see?" The Firemaker said.

"Yeeees! So much has happened! This adventure, the discoveries and victories – the insights about life in general! It's amazing! I'm still taking it all in, but things are making more and more sense and starting to come together."

"And how do you feel?"

"I'm a little shaky to be honest. That was a pretty rough ordeal. But I'm calm on the inside and, while I know it's hard to believe, I'm happy."

"Any other thoughts?"

"Well, I still feel horrible about a lot of things we humans do. I mean, the violence we perpetrate against each other is insane. It just makes me so upset and sad."

"But even that contains positives because my dissatisfaction is also what drives me to want to grow and make sure I'm not contributing to more darkness."

"And if I grow enough, I'll help change those things with my living. That feels so good."

"I've also realized that drawing quick conclusions based on the outcome of an individual or a collective act can be a mistake."

"This is like having new eyes. It's that simple."

The Firemaker nodded. "Go on."

Okay. Well, I've learned so much about personal will and how powerful it is in our lives, and about how, whether we realize it or not, we play a huge role in generating what we receive. I've learned that it's extremely easy to rant and rave about how bad things are, but what I need to concentrate on is how much I participate in creating my own experience.

"So, if I'm creating it, why don't I just stop complaining and start changing what I'm creating? That makes a whole lot more sense."

I paused for a moment, and then added, "I've also learned it's not that *easy* to give full attention to all that's actually going on."

"Yes, that's a large part of it. Anything else?"

"Absolutely! I feel so much better than I have for a long time. I feel like I did as a little girl. You know, in love with life!"

"Somewhere along the way I'd forgotten joy. I got lost in the Mists of Circumstance, struggling against life rather than letting myself go with it to my Downstream Dream of Wholeness where I truly want and need to be."

"And now?"

"Now I know the difference. And I know that I was living almost exclusively in my Lesser Self."

"So it's obvious that my choices were, by default, Lesser Self choices. I mean, what else could they have been, given the results? Simply knowing that one truth changes everything."

"It's challenging but also incredibly comforting. I don't feel utterly confused at the core. And you know what else? I'm starting to notice how beautiful things are. Little things that I used to take for granted, like a fallen leaf, or the true nature of fire. I realize now that I'd totally forgotten how to *see!* "

"You're blossoming, Helen, growing from the seed of your Lesser Self into the beautiful flower of your Greater Self."

"Thank you, Firemaker. I really am, aren't I?" I said, grinning broadly. "I'm starting to appreciate what that means."

The Firemaker nodded her head.

"You know, I almost called for you when I was in that little blue boat during the storm, but somewhere deep down inside I knew I'd be all right."

"Before traversing this latest door, I never thought so. Not really. Not like I do now. Clearly, I needed to discover these things for myself."

"Yes, Helen. You weathered the storm, as I knew you would, and you found the sweetness and joy of your Downstream Dream. As you claim it, you'll find aspects of your being waiting to be realized, and you'll begin to feel the wholeness and self-unification you've longed for."

"That sounds spiritual."

"Only if you want it to be. As we've discussed, your personal will determines what it means to you. For someone with a spiritual or even religious inclination, it becomes part of their nature. For someone who's not so inclined, or who's skeptical of such things, it's simply a scientific way of living. It works either way. I think you understand what I mean."

"Yes, I do. Even though I've absolutely, one hundred percent stumbled through, everything seems so clear now."

"I've learned that not resisting isn't the same thing as surrendering. I didn't really get that before."

"I had to surrender during the storm. I had no choice."

"But not resisting is an active choice. While I was waiting for the wind to bring me back to shore, I had to choose how I'd handle the waiting, the nothingness."

"I chose to still myself, to stay centered and allow things to happen around me...for me. It must have been a little like that for Peri and Virgie when their loved ones died."

"Yes, Helen" she said, pausing to allow what I shared to settle into my heart. "You're realizing what you're capable of, without outside help. You're beginning to understand that each door has been a new level of learning attained, and each experience another layer of your Pearl removed."

"Firemaker, I can hardly believe, even after all that's happened, that it's happened to me."

She laughed softly. "I know these experiences have been out of the ordinary, but for you to learn to adapt to rapidly changing circumstances without undue trauma, they've been absolutely necessary."

"Yes, Firemaker! All of this has been exactly what I needed. Now I feel like I can go freely toward what truly nourishes who I am."

"This *is* wonderful, Helen."

"I agree! But there's something that bothers me. Despite my newfound confidence, I'm still going to have doubts. I'm still going to be confused and afraid sometimes, especially about making decisions."

"That's never been easy for me, you know? When I have an important decision to make and there's more than one good choice, I get frazzled and crazy going round and round trying to figure out what to do."

"It's like I'm one of those silly hamsters on a treadmill scurrying nowhere as fast as their little legs can take them."

"Some of that's just life, Helen. There's always a little doubt. Even the truly great souls experience it. But now when you feel confused, you can remember the lesson, the door that corresponds to the experience you're having."

"It will be helpful for you to hold this journey as close as a dear companion who can help guide you through the rest of your life."

I thought for a moment. "Yes, knowing that I can recall the lessons, revisit the doors so to speak, is very reassuring. I like that. Sometimes life is messy and unclear, and deep down I know that's okay, but mostly I haven't been able to handle these kinds of messes very well."

"I guess, the truth is, personal will still makes me a little nervous. I feel like one of those new drivers, those rookie *soul drivers* you talked about before who bang into each other."

And now that I know how much power we have over our own lives because of our personal will, I can't help feeling like the whole thing is a huge responsibility."

"There's a reason you feel this way, Helen. Your Lesser Self still believes you'll choose poorly, make a mistake, be judged and have to pay for your error."

"Let me explain..."

CHAPTER 27

The Ring

The Firemaker paused, then said, "Unless there are immediate consequences to your actions, there's almost no way you can know with certainty if you've chosen well or chosen poorly."

I must have looked perplexed because she nodded and continued.

"Expecting that you'll be judged harshly for what you've chosen is part of a deeply ingrained belief come to you through your family from the time you were very young. It's a belief in your own badness. And the experiences that fed that belief formed the core elements of your Pearl."

"As a child, negative outcomes were the only way you knew if you'd acted appropriately or not. Punishment was your compass, Helen, one of the few reliable, though painful, ways for you to see how you were doing at any given moment."

"But you have a better compass now. You have a real and trustworthy method to find your way. You've discovered that the

City of Joy is the place inside of you where your Downstream Dream flows. And it's your Downstream Dream that will always be the most immediate, true compass in your life."

"When you make any decision that moves you closer to your Downstream Dream, you'll feel a sense of relief, rightness and calm. If circumstances or your actions take you upstream, and there may be times you'll have to go there briefly, you'll feel tense, tired and disconnected from what really makes life worth living."

"Remember the white powder that was left on the ground after you smashed your Pearl on Star Island?"

"I do!"

"Good, because it's an important symbol. You see, even though you've smashed your Pearl, and most of your pain and confusion has already dissipated, there will be residue surfacing for a while, maybe even for a long while. This is true for everyone who smashes their Pearls. And that's what you're experiencing right now when you doubt yourself."

"Maybe this example will help." she said.

I nodded. "Go on."

"A soldier has been wounded with shrapnel from the explosion of an artillery shell. Shrapnel from that blast has been deeply embedded in the soldier's tissues and will continue to work its way out of her body for many years."

"True, the soldier has lived through the initial explosion of the armament, or in this case, the Pearl, and the major source of damage has been destroyed, but that doesn't eliminate all of the smaller pockets of shrapnel that went deep into her physical or psychic body. Healing from that kind of damage doesn't happen all at once. It can take a long time for all of those experiences and feelings to come to the surface and be dealt with once and for all."

"Be patient with yourself when you're feeling as if you should be further along in your progress, Helen."

"Yes, you have accomplished, seen, and learned much. But residue from smashing your Pearl will still surface from time to time."

"When that happens, just remember, it's simply the shrapnel surfacing, and that's perfectly in line with the process required for growing beyond your past."

"Here," she said. "I'm going to give you something to help yourself when you feel confused."

The Firemaker pointed to the little bag hanging around my neck. "Open your pouch." The leather was supple as it had been before the storm. I reached inside and found the coin.

"Toss the coin into the air, Helen. Toss it high."

Summoning the same intensity I'd used to spin the Big Deal Wheel, I pitched the coin high into the air. As it rose higher and higher its center opened and began to expand. It was becoming a ring.

"Look up. What do you see inside of the ring?"

At first small enough to fit on my finger, the ring was growing larger as it ascended. Inside of it I saw the problems and difficulties I didn't know how to resolve. As I concentrated, the ring reached the apex of its arch and started to fall back down.

Then, "Quickly, Helen. Focus on one situation."

"That's a good choice," she said. "Now, untangle it from all of the other situations clamoring for your attention and look into the center of the ring. Look for the truth with your heart. When you find it, you'll know what to do."

I focused on the ring with all my might. So strong was my intention to see, so powerful my will to act, the ring abruptly stopped falling several feet above my head, where it stayed, hovering in the air just slightly beyond my reach.

"What do you see?"

"I see the situation as it is by itself, without a bunch of other stuff clouding it. I can feel and see things about it that I couldn't before."

"I know what I need to do!!"

"Excellent. Don't tell me, just put it in your heart for later."

"Now take the ring."

I had to stretch onto the very tips of my toes to reach it. In the last moment before I took hold, I lost my balance. The ring began to fall and I had to lunge to grab it.

"Good catch, Helen. What do you see now?"

"I see just exactly what's been blocking me deep down, beneath all the static about what I should do and how I should feel."

Then the ring flattened out and became a coin again. By now too much had happened for me to marvel at the transformation. I slipped it back into the pouch as I gathered my thoughts.

"Do you know what you'll do now?"

"Yes, Firemaker, I do. Choosing one thing to focus on by putting the ring around it helped me to let all of the other problems go – for just a moment. And in that moment I saw the truth and I knew what I wanted."

"I also saw that my habit of gathering problems together and worrying over them all at the same time only exhausted and confused me."

"The little details and upsets I have about each situation get all tangled up and I can't see my way through. But I've got it now. I need to look at each situation by itself and draw a little ring around it in *the center of my heart*."

"Yes, that's right. Anything else?"

"I must consider which Self is involved in the seeing."

"Very good, Helen. Excellent."

"It's always my Lesser Self that's confused, isn't it?"

The Firemaker nodded.

It's that Baby Self. It just doesn't want to give up on wanting things to be a certain way. When I chose the problem I focused on, I suddenly realized I'd been hoping for a different outcome than the one I really needed.

"I wasn't letting my Greater Self guide me or the Baker prepare and deliver the loaf. I was keeping myself from the truth, and that was preventing me from knowing what to do."

"The Firemaker nodded again and then turned, pointing toward the west."

"You've done extremely well through the first six doors. I think you're ready to finish your journey now, Helen. Am I right about that?"

I smiled and didn't hesitate. "Yes, Firemaker. I most certainly am."

CHAPTER 28

The Choice

I might have thought I was ready to finish, but The Firemaker was about to throw me a curve ball. She pointed to a little path and said, "That way to the last door. Go ahead. I'll follow."

We walked for a minute or two, turned a corner, and came to a fork. The path continued to trail for a few yards, and then abruptly ended, each one with a door.

"What!" I cried, stunned. "You told me there were seven doors! I see *two* and that makes eight!"

"Helen, what I said was you needed to *pass through* seven doors. I never indicated that there weren't more than seven."

I shielded my eyes from the sun, scrutinizing each of the two doors. Neither had a tile, but when I concentrated, one door flashed the image of a candle in a cave, and the other of a lotus flower in the center of a flame.

"So, I guess all that stuff about how to choose comes into play right here and now, huh?"

"Yes, Helen, it does," said The Firemaker, with a smile in her voice.

"Okay, I know I can do this," I said under my breath, and then a little louder, "I can do this!" And then I reached into the pouch and took out the coin, turning it to the face with the word, *inside*.

Tumbling it in my fingers, I gave myself a pep talk. "This isn't about your whole life, Helen, all your problems, where you've been or what you might have done better. It's about making a choice, the best one you can, right now, in this moment. If you don't like the outcome you can always course correct and find another way to approach the situation."

With that I flipped the coin into the air and saw it expand once more into a ring. In an instant I saw the lotus in the flame and knew without a doubt which door I had to pick.

As the realization came to me, the ring returned to its original state and dropped neatly into my hand.

I smiled at The Firemaker and with no qualms walked up the path and stepped squarely in front of the door I'd chosen.

I'm going in here," I said confidently.

Then I opened the Seventh Door.

CHAPTER 29

The Seventh Door

It's difficult to explain how sure I was that this was my door, but in some deep way I can't really name, I felt infinitely strong as I stepped through. I knew I belonged there, and I expected to be bowled over by something utterly magical on the other side.

After all, this was my seventh and last door. Unfortunately it wasn't all that magical. Far from it.

Instead of the fabulous finale I'd imagined, I stepped knee deep into a nasty, foul-smelling swamp...stubbed my toe on something under the water...and fell face down into the muck.

"What the????" I shouted, covered from head to toe in black mud and some kind of creepy vines.

"Great! So much for my choosing abilities! I chose the Crap Door!!!"

Just then, a voice croaked: "Maybe not. Maybe not. Maybe not."

"What? Who...who said that?" I heard a huge *ker-splash*! Then, a frog the size of a football landed on a rotting log right next to my leg. "I said it! I said it! I said it!"

"Well, who the heck are you?" I demanded.

"Tour guide. Tour guide. Tour guide."

"Tour guide. What kind of dismal tour is this?"

"Tour of the past. Tour of the past. Tour of the past."

I shook my head and wiped as much mud off my face with both hands as I could. "Why am I not surprised?" Having been through so much before, I finally had to laugh at this mess.

By this time, I'd long since realized that the Land Behind the Doors could hold *anything,* and that sooner or later, so far anyway, it all ended up making sense.

"Okay, I'm game. Lemme have it."

"Walk to the end. Walk to the end. Walk to the end," the frog said.

I looked around. The water was greasy and thick with snaking vines and all kinds of floating debris, but there seemed to be only one possible way to move, so I started in that direction.

"This way, I assume?"

The frog hunkered down, and I could see that he was about ready to spring.

"That's the way. That's the way. That's the way," he croaked. Then he lifted off for parts unknown and disappeared.

"Some tour guide," I muttered.

With no other obvious options, I slogged along for what felt like hours. But it didn't take long to discover that inside this ugly swamp was all that I'd ever worried about or feared would come to pass – to me and to the world. These were the things I'd hoped to leave behind but dreaded would revisit me sooner or later because, essentially, I was all messed up and deserved it.

Clearly this was part of the residue, the shrapnel left over from smashing my Pearl as The Firemaker had explained.

It was awful. More than awful. Drums of chemical waste as big as linebackers pushed up against empty plastic bottles and other wretched and abandoned things I couldn't identify.

A mass of corroded electrical wires had nested inside a rusty bedspring abloom with mold and the wayward companions of a child's life. A miniature donkey with two holes in her back where a ribbon ran through and a faded blue Teddy Bear with one eye and no mouth had become snagged in the coils, Teddy's little flannel vest hitching them a ride to nowhere.

My stomach leapt into my chest, squeezing my heart and throat so hard I couldn't make a sound. I reached for Donkey and Blue, my tiny counselors in a long forgotten room filled with the terrified tears of a warrior child who never let go of hope.

I tried to get to them, but the more I pushed the more stuck I became. I was in the Swamp of my Past, all right, up to my armpits in despair, knee deep in the rotting tonnage of human upstream struggles.

As hard as I tried I could not save Donkey and Blue. So I thanked them for all they witnessed and believed when no one else would. They'd come with me into the curtain-drawn room where bad things happened, until I realized there would be no rescue from Tuesdays other than what my own brave heart could make happen.

There was more to this place than my own dark past. Heavy with the slime of decay and the bloated ghosts of longing, disappointment, and loss, the swamp was a watershed clogged with the obsolete and hidden waste of generations and the ancient anguish of the world. A legion of Lesser Self desires and decades of Beehives and human soul sickness had turned this once-clean water foul. All I wanted was out, but that would not come quickly.

As I stood and took it all in, a tiny light began to blink at me over the water from far away. Then there was another, and then another tiny light flashing toward me through the gloom.

I became giddy with hope as tears welled up in my eyes, or maybe it was just sweat, and suddenly everything started to become blurry.

"You've come a long way," said Lucy, the first firefly to arrive, her voice soft as the caress of a summer breeze.

"Things aren't always what they seem, Miss Helen," trilled the next and smallest firefly with a showy twirl of her iridescent wings.

"I'm Nell," she squeaked, wiggling her belly light to the right. "That was Lucy."

"And I'm Mae," crooned the third and largest firefly, her voice as soothing as rain after midnight.

"Best to reset to neutral if you can," Mae continued.

"That's right," chimed Nell. "The earth has always been round."

"And water always returns to the sea," whispered luminous Lucy, sparkling extra brightly.

CHAPTER 30

The Pool of Possible Futures

As soon as they'd arrived, the fireflies were on their way. But their words would not leave me. No matter how foul or narrow flowing, all water returns to the ocean. Coming home over or through the land, it will eventually make its way back. For you see, it's never really separate from its wholeness. Everything returns to source. That's the nature of things.

Nell was right. Even with all the enormous darkness in the world, we have come a long way and the past can open doors to growth and healing if we allow ourselves to make new choices.

I couldn't give up now.

After what seemed like forever in that twilight hell, I heard the sound of rushing water. The thought of being able to wash off the muck of the swamp gave me renewed energy and I pressed on.

Soon, I could see a little stream running off the edge of a cliff high above, and a beautiful crystal waterfall about a hundred yards from where the swamp dried up and turned into a muddy bank.

With some real effort, I extricated myself from the swamp and mud, ran to the little waterfall and dove straight under it. The icy water was invigorating, and I scrubbed myself with every ounce of energy I had. I wanted it off of me and washing it away felt so good I couldn't help but giggle.

While I was bathing, I spied a lovely meadow no more than a half-mile away. When I was clean, I headed directly for it. As I walked, the air was sweet and cool against my skin, and the long summer grass moved like ribbons in the wind pointing toward the horizon and beyond.

On the way to the meadow, I realized that every door, including this one, had been challenging and exhausting, but ultimately exhilarating, even if it took a while for the positive feelings to set in. And though I hadn't chosen it, I had no end of curiosity about what was behind the *other* door, the one picturing the candle in the cave. Just a little peek would have been nice, you know?

Still, I knew I was in the right place, especially after having passed through the Swamp of the Past and the Purifying Waterfall. It took me awhile, but at last I was done with all that pain and darkness.

It was warm in the meadow and the quiet afternoon sounds of insects and birds made me so relaxed and drowsy I lay down to rest. Just at the edge of my awareness, as I hovered between sleeping and waking, a vision rolled into my mind like the gauzy end of a dream.

The images that came to me were completely different from the ones I'd seen in the Auditorium. These were wonderful and they brought me deep into the center of my heart and possibilities I'd never allowed myself to think of as more than fantasies and wishes.

In *this* vision, I was surrounded by people who loved me and whom I loved deeply. I was strong, happy and fulfilled, like a sun-drenched flower opening to the light that embraced and surrounded it, like the air of The Garden.

This was how my life could be, and it was available to me from the blueprint of my own dreams and the deepest desires of my soul. All I had to do was choose.

When I opened my eyes, I saw something I hadn't noticed before. Just a few feet away where the grass thinned, there was a gentle path leading to a small pool filled with clear turquoise water.

Intuitively I knew that this was where I was supposed to go, and I got up and walked toward it. When I reached the pool, I waded without hesitation into the shallow end, and then moved in further to where the water was chest-high. I was so lost in my joy that I was surprised and a little bewildered to hear, "Does that feel good to you, Helen?"

"Wha...? Oh, yes, Firemaker! Almost unbearably good."

"This, Helen, is the Pool of Possible Futures. Made from Universal Ether, it's filled with all of the wonderful futures longed for in your heart of hearts. It is *The Pool of Life*."

"The Swamp of the Past is its complete opposite, and made from the personal and collective darkness of humanities' most negative beliefs, ones that only a short time ago you claimed daily through your thoughts of fear, negation and lack."

"You're free to choose the reality in which you swim. Regardless of appearances, regardless of how dire a situation seems – everyone is free to make that choice, although most never know it."

"As you make your choice, be sure to remember that what you believe has more impact on your life than you've ever imagined. You have the power to create your future, Helen. Name what you want and claim it. Choose who you truly are and be it."

I thought for a moment. This was exhilarating stuff, but sobering, too. If I understood The Firemaker correctly, we're all in a constant state of creating, and it begins with what we create inside.

Whether I viewed it scientifically, psychologically or extended it into the realm of religion and spirituality, truth was still truth. I'd have to be in one place or the other, the Pool of Possible Futures or the Swamp of the Past. Which one I ended up in was up to me.

"Shall I go on?" The Firemaker asked.

I swam a little closer to her and said, "Yes, Firemaker, please do."

"Very well. There will be more choices, and you will find yourself on a path with a particular ending in mind. What you've just learned has many practical applications, even the process of goal attainment. That might be something of importance to you now that you have a direction, yes?"

I smiled, and nodded. Yes, indeed. I was on a path, moving forward toward my wonderful possible futures.

"Yes? Then let's say you're proceeding toward a goal – something challenging yet full of heart, like earning a degree, writing a book or transforming a harmful behavior into something that helps you to thrive. It could be anything you felt called to achieve, like gaining physical strength or mastering a new skill."

"Once you've fully seen what you desire in your mind, the process is to allow yourself to flow backwards through the stages of development that will deliver it up. By doing whatever common sense and practical guidelines say you must do to finish, if you direct your will and don't falter, you will achieve your goal and become what you envision, because what you envision, if it is a *goal of your heart*, is on some level already true."

"And it begins with your Downstream Dream, with realizing what you would look like, at the end, believing that you have the ability to be what you dream and to live the life that dream makes possible."

"There is no more need for despair, Helen. Now you have a pathway to your dreams. It's a living thing and you will create it as you see fit and move forward to the destination of your Downstream Dream of Wholeness."

Yes! Oh yes!! I would grow and I would allow myself to bloom into whatever I chose to become. "I understand, Firemaker," I said as I lowered my body deeper into the Pool. It was exquisite and I knew without a doubt that I had definitely chosen the correct Seventh Door.

CHAPTER 31

Footprints

Deep in thought, I floated in the Pool recalling everything that had happened, all the learning and new understandings that came with each door. I felt as if I could stay in the Pool forever, just existing. But I also knew that, as sweet and glorious as it was, there was more, much more, to do. There was a whole new life to be lived.

A little flutter in my heart told me there was something more for me to see and I knew it was terribly important.

By now I'd come to accept what that meant. As amazing as new vision is, it rarely seems to come without a good bit of roll-up-your-sleeves hard work.

"There will always be more to learn, Helen," The Firemaker said. "Perhaps what you're feeling is the need to gather your experiences together from the perspective of where you are now, while it's still fresh. This may be a good time for us to revisit the doors."

"Yes," I said. "That sounds right."

CHAPTER 32

The Seven Doors

The Firemaker asked, "Where should we begin?"

"Well, I guess it makes sense to start at the beginning"

"To the First Door, then," she said, nodding.

"While you were in the Amusement Park, most of the people you noticed, the ones spinning for personal gain, were there because of something called *Generalized Longing*."

"They were looking for something to take the ache of that longing away."

"Unfortunately, unless a person has awakened to their Greater Self, the Wheel can bring more entanglement than freedom, and the prizes it generates obscure rather than fulfill the core truths of the heart."

"To be really finished with the need to revisit such a place, one must know what she truly wants. But that knowing isn't always so easy to discern. Often what one thinks she needs doesn't turn out to be what she thought it was or where she thought she would find it."

"Many of the people at the Wheel had no idea about their Downstream Dream. Without knowing one's true destination, it's not possible to ever be truly happy, at peace and fulfilled in life."

Her words, though not wholly unfamiliar, had an energizing effect, like an unexpected cool breeze on a warm day. Hearing them now inspired a larger vision. There was a reason my journey had begun at the Wheel.

I was beginning to understand that each of my lessons grew out of that one and joined to the next in a deeply purposeful way. This wasn't just about me. It wasn't just about my journey. It was about *all* of us.

The bigger picture was starting to come into focus.

"Helen, in order for you to find your Downstream Dream, you had to stop spinning the Wheel. It's the only way to move beyond the perpetual cycles of Generalized Longing."

"Then you had to confront the specific nature of your wound, the primal event or events where a part of you became stuck. That's what the people behind the Second Door, in the Auditorium, were doing."

"It was in the Auditorium that you gained insight into your wound and the wounds of others. That's where you discovered the importance of letting the *wound identity* go when it takes on enough mass to become a Pearl."

"You also saw how your Pearl had engulfed and obscured something you'd had inside all along – *Your piece of the sun!* After that you came to realize the necessity of looking at others and yourself and all of life through compassionate eyes."

"Behind the Third Door you saw how the wound plays out in relationships. When you found the Beehive, you had a great shock and came to know that sometimes those who have been hurt also sting."

"Do you remember what the beekeeper told you just before she left?"

"To wear a protective suit if I was going to go toward the hive, or even be around bees for that matter. Right?"

The Firemaker nodded. "Yes, a suit to protect you from being stung. But, as you know, that's no simple task. Dealing with bees can be a dangerous business. As you discovered, the hive can be a place or it can live on inside of people long after they've left it. There are many ways that one can find themselves in hive territory.

"But what's most important, Helen, is to know that the more one is stung, the less resistant one becomes to the effect, though the desire for what bees offer doesn't seem to lessen, at least not easily. And with enough stings, the body becomes allergic and eventually even a small amount of their poison can overwhelm the system."

"It was essential for you to see what the Beehive represents and that being stung not only hurts, it can eventually make you ill or even take your life away."

"Knowing that, and with the victory of walking away from the hive *because your gut told you to*, you saw that any relationship can contain sweetness or stings, and that some contain both."

"And if you can't devise a suit for the ones with stings," I said, "then you have to be smart enough and strong enough to walk away, *no matter who the person is*."

"Yes, Helen," the Firemaker said, nodding and smiling.

"And with that awareness it was easy for you to learn the lesson of the Fourth Door, Sugar and the Diner, and to shift your perception to the idea that wholeness comes from inside of *you*, not in the form of two at the expense of one."

"Relationships with other people are essential to healthy living, but only if the people involved are standing on an equal, visible, agreed-upon common base."

"Those experiences prepared you well for the Fifth Door, where you found the Bakery and learned about the complexity of your Subconscious Mind, your Lesser Self and Greater Self, and of the ultimate destination, integration into a Unified Spirit."

"With that knowledge, you entered the Sixth Door and boarded the little blue boat to face your biggest challenge – a lifelong fear of the water."

"Alone, you found the strength to survive the storm and make your way to Star Island where the actions you took changed everything. When you smashed your Pearl, you found your piece of the sun, something you've been looking for *all your life*. And when you held it, you knew that the City of Joy lives inside of you."

"That was your awakening, and when it came time for the Seventh Door, you drew from within, took the coin from the pouch and beheld its transformation into a circle of discernment."

"Another difficult choice, but you stepped forward, once again, into the unknown. And as with each door, you encountered a setback, or at least what appeared to be a setback."

"But, you pushed ahead, so much so that when you came to the Pool your decision was obvious and instantaneous. Without reservation you chose to go ahead and pointed yourself in the direction of the wonderful Possible Futures awaiting you."

"You've done beautifully, Helen. Really you have. With each door you reclaimed another part of your wholeness. With each challenge you embraced, you activated another inner resource, one of so many inside of you."

CHAPTER 33

The Teachers Behind The Doors

I felt as light and free as a butterfly in springtime, and I told The Firemaker so. We enjoyed the moment. And when I was ready, she shared this...

"Inner emptiness is a lot like a low tide, Helen. No matter the water level, the ocean is still the ocean. *You* are no less whole in times of lack. When life doesn't bring forth the conditions one requires to thrive, there is no diminishment of self, no not-wholeness."

"And gathering more to one's self, be it food or any manner of external stimulations, will not make you more whole, no matter how wonderfully expansive the sensation. Such paths to igniting your Life Force are fleeting at best, and tend to take more than they give. Being full is not the same as being whole. It's not the same as making a fire of your own."

A wave of something electric went through me and I remembered what Lucy had told me when I was lost in the terrible Swamp of the Past.

"It's wise, Helen, to remember what you learned from the teachers behind the doors."

"Teachers? You mean like the fireflies? Sugar? And the Beekeeper?"

"Yes, and there were others, too. More than you think. You might want to look again at those you encountered along the way, at what they were doing behind each door, and why they were there."

"Why they were there? For their pain, right?"

"Yes," she nodded. "Many of the people at the Wheel came to spin because somewhere inside they knew their *lives* weren't whole. Others spun for noble purposes, like relieving another's pain, and some spun to relieve their own."

"Some of the people in the Auditorium were ready to admit to themselves that something was terribly wrong with staying where they were. Others were content to stay in the City of Stability. But all had arrived because of their pain."

"And the women who were so desperate for the sweetness of the hive that they kept going in unprepared, pretending that the bees wouldn't hurt them?"

"Yes, Helen, like those Sugar waits on who look to the drug of romantic love to fill them up and ease their hurt. In the end, all that running around is only a distraction, or worse, a path to being dominated or abused by another partner or situation."

"As Sugar explained, that doesn't mean one should be afraid of love or of entering into new settings and experiences; what it does mean is that one should go in with eyes wide open."

"Many experiences come with living. Some, on th' end of the continuum, are merely unpleasant, whi ones that seem hardest to let go of, are dangerou., threatening, like one bee sting too many."

"A human being can only take so much injury before they become ill, in body *or* mind. It may occur little by little, or in one shattering moment from a tragically false step or poorly navigated decision driven by shame or inner pain, or perhaps by some other unforeseen event."

"The experiences build upon each other, as you have seen, much like the gritty layers of a Pearl growing inside an oyster."

"When one repeatedly perceives that she is inadequate, a kind of deep inner confusion sets in. It can reach the point where she can even forget her true nature and that she is the creator of the Pearl and not the Pearl itself."

"Regardless of what name one might give it, ultimately it's the sadness of not being loved that was at the center of your Pearl, Helen. But now you know that you're worthy of all you dream. And you have the eyes to see that this is true because you've worked to strip away the false ideas and beliefs crystallized at the deepest levels of your being."

"You've smashed your Pearl and are nearly set free because of it. But there's one more piece you must have to complete your transformation from internal bondage to freedom."

CHAPTER 34

The Secret

"Helen, if you can convert what I am about to say into awareness, there's nothing you cannot unlock, including relationships, your career, spirituality, all of it. It's the key that opens many of the mysteries of life."

The Firemaker motioned toward the back of the Pool. As I shifted my focus I saw each of the seven doors I had passed through. They were set side by side, embedded into an ancient, vine-covered stone wall. Each door had one word printed beneath the tile and together they formed this sentence...

ALL ILLNESS COMES FROM A BROKEN HEART

There it was. Seven little words clearing up what had haunted me for so long. With an elegant, simple stroke, The Firemaker had shown me why I had to make it through seven doors, not five or even six. It must be *seven* or *The Secret of the Broken Heart* would be incomplete.

She was showing me the story of my life and handing me the key to everything that had dogged me, everything I'd never understood about myself, or my parents, or my loves or anyone else.

Now so very clear, I could actually see the pathway of lived-through pain that connected the outer to the inner and the past to the present. I would never again be able to deny or ignore that I knew this.

I would never be able to pretend, as I had done before I began my journey, that walking around with a broken heart had nothing to do with how I felt or the choices I'd made. It had everything to do with it. Nor could I deny that everybody who intentionally inflicts pain on this planet is suffering from an illness and has a broken heart, too.

"Remember The Secret of the Broken Heart, keep it well and you will bring great healing into the world."

"All illness comes from a broken heart, Helen. When you're ready to share what you now know, there will be people who say it's not so...that it applies only to certain situations, or is little more than a fanciful way to talk about personal pain. No matter. It *IS* the truth, and not just for one whose life transparently reveals the source of their pain. It is the answer to that which you have been seeking, inside yourself and the whole of the world."

"Doing harm is an illness, and it comes from a broken heart. And on Earth at this time, it is a pandemic, an invisible illness that afflicts virtually everyone, victim or perpetrator. And so it has been for thousands of years."

"This is the answer to your Big Why. The madness of murder, war, and other darkness on this planet is an illness that travels through a chain of broken hearts linked by time and lineage so far distant that the memory of the beginning exists only in myths and the history written on gravestones and in books."

I felt strangely dizzy, as if the axis of my personal universe had just shifted. And I guess it had. At last I understood what had been wrong with me, as The Firemaker had said, all those long, lonely years. It was a moment of clarity and great relief as I felt my sadness, so heavy and so constant, lift and dissipate like fog in the warm sun.

Something bound deep in the middle of me released and spiraled out through the palms of my hands and feet as if an enormous bell had been struck, ringing one long, clear, clean tone throughout the cells of my body, charging them with light and the energy of freedom.

Now I understood myself, and why I'd so desperately needed to know how so much pain could exist in such a beautiful world. Yet there was something still troubling me and I had to get it right before I could move on.

"I understand, Firemaker. The thing is, you said *all illness*, not just some illness. So, by illness I'm thinking you mean *all* disharmony in people, and on the planet, yes?"

The Firemaker nodded.

I nodded back. "Well then, what about when babies are born with physical or mental limitations? They didn't experience a broken heart and end up in that condition."

"No, of course not. So we must look beyond *apparent reality* for the understanding. The answer to your question comes in two parts: First, the Secret doesn't say that the broken heart that causes the illness has to be *yours*. In cases of genetic conditions, the broken heart may have been that of the great-great-great-great grandmother or grandfather of the child."

"But the point at which the genetic changes took place introducing illness into the family line, it came from a broken heart."

"Second, a parent or parents can attract illness to a child out of worry, dread or an imagination that focuses on danger and harm coming to the baby. Parents can draw these things to their children, and the parents' fears that result in the child's illness *always* come from a broken heart."

"So you're saying that sometimes children are just stuck with something from birth and nothing can change that?"

"Certainly for many children the destruction caused by a broken heart, or a chain of broken hearts in one's genealogy, can have such impact that it's almost impossible to overcome. It shapes the child's environment to such an extent that his or her biggest challenge will be to cope with it. But in spite of that, great accomplishments have come from people who were burdened by tremendous physical challenges."

"Some well-known examples are the hearing loss of Edison and Beethoven. Both were deaf. I'm sure you can think of dozens more."

"Yes, I see it clearly now. I've always wondered why children with seemingly loving parents suffer and fall ill in tragic, inexplicable ways when they haven't had a chance like the rest of us to even start getting into trouble. It seems so unjust. But as you've taught me, I need to resist making hasty conclusions and judgments."

"That's right, and as we've discussed, from the human perspective a lot of existence at this level has some very cruel edges. Would you like to stop, to perhaps reflect on this?"

I thought for a moment, "No, thank you, Firemaker. I'm okay. This fills in a lot of blanks."

"Truthfully, I guess I thought I was done with these kinds of questions. But up until now most of them have been outwardly focused. I wasn't allowing myself to look at the really personal, painful stuff. As you said way back after the Second Door, pain comes off the way it goes on, in layers."

"Now that I know The Secret of the Broken Heart, it's plain to see how small I've been, and why I've lived such a mediocre existence when all along there were so many other incredible possibilities I could have chosen."

"My broken heart is mending, Firemaker. I never want to forget The Secret or the Lessons of the Doors. Never."

"You won't forget, Helen. You could choose to ignore what you've experienced, but you will never forget what you have learned. It has become a part of you and will go forward with you as you create your future. That's what you've gained the ability to do, you see."

"You've earned the right to possess The Secret of the Broken Heart. That gives you the power to choose your most appropriate future and create it."

"The doors you've passed through and The Secret written on them are your guides. Remember their lessons and your heart will never be so easily broken again."

I sighed and nodded, feeling a soft, inner calm blooming from within. Yes, *the heart can heal the heart*. And my heart, if not completely unbreakable, was resilient, strong, and incredibly alive. I was no longer lost in a fog and vulnerable. I'd come home to the inside of me where my little piece of the sun had always lived. I was whole and I was free.

I smiled at the woman in the robe, her still hidden face a familiar and welcome sight.

CHAPTER 35

The Face of The Firemaker

"Firemaker, will I ever be allowed to see your face?"

She laughed gently. "Certainly, Helen. Now that you have passed through seven doors, you can see my face anytime you like."

I swallowed hard. "Now?"

"Now is the perfect time. Look into the surface of the water."

Looking into the pool, now mirror still, I saw only my own reflection. There were no other images anywhere on the surface, no clouds, no trees, nothing. Just me.

I looked up at The Firemaker and said, "I'm afraid I don't understand."

"Oh yes, Helen, you do. Somewhere inside you always have. "

Now, very slowly The Firemaker pulled back her hood. I gasped as once again, I was looking at *my own face.*

But it was my own face transformed. There were no worry lines or shadows. My skin was full of life and color, and my eyes clear and bright as mountain spring water.

"I am the embodiment of your Unified Self. What you have seen in me is what you will eventually become by connecting *all that is in you to all that you are to be.* There's still a long journey ahead to reach that place, but you will arrive there eventually.

"For now you've led yourself to yourself and now *you* are The Firemaker. Whenever you need to know what to do, remember the coin and the ring, and say these words..."

"I Am The Firemaker"

I drew in a deep breath, completely overcome by what was taking place.

"Say the words now, Helen, and assume your true place in life."

I knew that what The Firemaker was saying was vital, yet it was so overwhelming and profound I could barely summon the courage.

But then, remembering all the doors I'd passed through, all the tests I'd undertaken and The Secret of the Broken Heart, I took in another deep breath, seized the moment and spoke the words aloud, albeit in a whisper...

"I Am The Firemaker."

As the last, hushed word fell from my lips, her shimmering red gown dropped, empty, to the grass, in a heap.

I stared in disbelief, hardly breathing. Swimming slowly to the edge of the Pool, I pulled myself up and stood cautiously where my guide and teacher had stood. I called out to her, but she was gone. I was alone.

I stared at the gown, wanting to try it on but half expecting to be vaporized if I even touched it. That fleeting thought was immediately erased though, by my rapidly growing feeling of wellbeing.

When I finally reached for it a surge of indescribable warmth came over me and I suddenly remembered the smell of cinnamon, and oranges, and roses, and the Red Fairy who came to me in the night with her glowing, ruby-gold light.

At last I stepped into the gown and pulled it up around my shoulders. It fit flawlessly and felt wonderful against my bare skin. I shuddered with contentment.

As the gown settled around me, every muscle relaxed and I became aware of the little pouch that held the coin. I quickly opened it. It was a ring again, only this time exactly fitted to my finger. And on the outside, inscribed...*I Am The Firemaker.*

Images of Virgie and Peri's hands flashed through my mind and I instantly knew the ring belonged on the middle finger of my right hand, just as they wore theirs. I slipped it on and pulled the hood up over my hair.

The moment I donned the hood, a beautiful white lotus emerged from the Pool and burst into a magnificent flame of reds, yellows, blues and purples. The flame was bright, warm and alive, but it didn't consume or scorch the lotus and I knew that the fire was a living, eternal thing.

The flame was mesmerizing and enveloping, and then there was the feeling of being inside a giant kaleidoscope.

Everything was sparkling, moving, changing, and I was changing, too. It was dizzying.

The Seven Doors, the people I'd met, the knowledge and insights I'd gained, every moment of it flashed through my mind like lightning. I was transported into the air and floated above the scene of my bicycle accident. I was in it and yet not in it, an observer with no needs or wants, contented in a way I'd never felt before. Centered.

I saw myself lying by the roadside, dressed in my gardening clothes. My bicycle was on its side just a few inches away from my head.

I was wonderfully lucid. I knew who and where I was. And I knew that this was reality, and that what I'd just experienced at the Pool was reality, too.

I watched as an ambulance arrived and two paramedics hurried out of the truck and over to my body, checked my vital signs and looked me over.

They put a collar around my neck and gingerly loaded me onto a gurney and into the back of the truck. As they sped away, I floated above the vehicle as it raced through the streets and into the parking lot of a hospital emergency room.

I felt myself falling toward my body and lost consciousness again. I don't know how much time elapsed, but when I woke up, I was on a bed in the emergency room, groggy and aching, yet knowing that I was not seriously hurt. The emergency medical technicians from the truck were still there, along with a doctor and two nurses.

The doctor flashed her small light into my eyes and said, "Welcome back, Helen. We just need to take a look at your labs to make sure, but so far it doesn't look like there's anything wrong with you that a day or two of rest won't cure."

The hospital staff busied themselves with whatever it was they were doing to me, checking for broken bones or other injuries, I guess. A nurse handed the doctor some X-rays and she walked into another room to have a look.

Just then, one of the team who'd taken care of me spoke, "You doin' okay, Helen?"

I smiled, "Yeah – I'm okay I think. Kinda woozy. My head hurts like crazy."

She nodded. "I would imagine. That was a heck of a thump you took against that curb. But you look pretty good, goose egg and all."

"And the little girl with the soccer ball, is she okay? "

"Absolutely. You missed her by a mile. She's just fine. "

"Thank goodness for that."

"Well, we'd better get out of doc's way and back on the road. Oh, this is Nathan and I'm Lupita. Sorry about the circumstances, but it was still nice to meet you. Take good care."

I nodded back. "Yes, I will. Nice meeting you guys, too. Thank you both so much for helping me."

"Nothing to it. It's what we do." Lupita said with a wave.

Nathan waved, too, then suddenly stopped and came back over. By the way, we found Peri's name and address on a check in your wallet. We gave her a call and she should be here soon. Hope that's okay. We couldn't find any other contacts for you.

"Oh good, I'm glad she's coming. Peri's my boss, and my best friend. Thank you, Nathan."

"No problem, Helen. Like Lupita said, take good care. I hope you feel better real soon."

I watched them walk away. And while I don't know what it was exactly, maybe a whisper in my heart, but I was sure that something new had begun.

And I knew if that proved to be true, my journey behind the Doors had equipped me to handle it like a grown up. There would be no more *Protos* for me. I'd left *that* room a long time ago and was in a new one, a much better one, I was sure of it.

As Lupita and Nathan stepped out of the sliding glass doors I impulsively reached for the pouch around my neck. Gone. A touch of disappointment stabbed me, but I caught myself and refused to drop into that scared, childish place, my Lesser Self.

I remembered exactly what to do and whispered, "I Am The Firemaker."

The words brought a perfect sense of completion, strength and integration with my new consciousness. In the deepest center of my being, where the Greater Self resides, I knew the wisdom I'd been shown was the sure remedy to any petty fear my Lesser Self might conjure up.

I was The Firemaker now, and I knew I always would be. It was unnecessary, no, impossible, to go back to my old life, and I knew it. I felt wonderful!

I was whole and lit up from within by a piece of the sun as bright as the one I'd searched for so many years ago as a child.

When I looked up Peri was standing over me, studying my face, concerned but smiling. I smiled, too, and held out my left hand.

The emergency room lights were very bright behind her and I shielded my eyes with my right hand, glimpsing the gold ring on my middle finger.

"Good Lord, honey. That was sure a nasty spill. Look at that goose egg on your noggin. Are you okay?"

I beamed and clutched her hand tighter. "Better than ever, Peri."

The doctor, who had walked into the other room briefly, came back. "Your X-rays look good, Helen. Nothing broken. Just a mild concussion. If you feel like it, we can let you go home as long as you don't drive."

"I'll drive her back over to my place," Peri said. "Keep a watchful eye and make sure she takes it easy. I'll pamper her like one of my orchids." The doctor nodded. "Sounds good. Don't go to sleep for about three or four hours. Unless your headache worsens, there's nothing for you to do really. Just check back in with us next week. Take it easy for a couple of days, Helen. You'll be as good as new."

I smiled. "Thank you, doctor. Thanks so much for everything."

I stood up and, even though my head hurt and I was a little wobbly, I felt healthy, safe and strong. Peri steadied me as we went through the hospital doors and got into the car.

Outside, the rainstorm had passed and the sun was breaking out from behind marshmallow puffy clouds. It seemed to me as though I had never, in my whole life, seen such a stunning, heavenly display.

Peri put her arm around me, her intelligent brown eyes wide with love. "The paramedics told me they'd asked the man in the house near where you crashed to look after Dolly. You want to swing by and put her in the trunk, or would that be too much for you right now?"

"I'd like that. Dolly's my friend, so sure, let's go get her."

Peri drove us over and a nice, elderly gentleman went into his garage and rolled Dolly out.

"Looks like it's in pretty good shape," he said, loading her into the trunk.

"Haven't seen one of these old Huffy's since my kids were kids. How are you doing, young lady? Are you all right?"

"Yes, thanks, I'm fine, Mr.??"

"Saul. Call me Saul."

Nice to meet you, Saul. It's nothing a couple of days' rest won't cure. Thank you so much for looking after Dolly for me. I really appreciate it. It's Helen, by the way."

"You bet, Helen. Not a problem. Hope you're feeling better soon," he said with a wave, and walked back into his house.

Peri started the car and we headed for her place just a few blocks away.

"If I'm not mistaken, that was one powerful ride you were on."

I looked into those warm, keen eyes and instantly knew she was aware of my entire journey and that she'd taken some version of it herself.

And I also knew that Virgie was a Firemaker, Peri was a Firemaker, and so was I. Sisters all.

"Yes, very powerful, Peri. Pivotal and powerful."

Then I remembered the two little tiles Peri had given me in the potting shed the day before.

Quickly I dug into my backpack, not quite certain what I would find. Inside, there was only one tile and sure enough, it was the one with the lotus and flame. I wasn't a bit surprised. The tile with the candle in the cave was not mine, at least not now.

Maybe it would be later, or maybe never. It didn't matter. I knew that I'd chosen the perfect Seventh Door, and that soon Peri and I would cement the lotus and flame tile to the last altar in the garden.

I felt like laughing out loud with happiness but simply smiled and said. "Well, Peri, this was a much needed little bump on the head." I paused to think for a moment. "This tile is the last one for the garden, if that's okay with you. I'm afraid I misplaced the other one."

"Misplaced, huh?" Peri chuckled. "Yes, this tile is perfect. Good choice, Helen. We'll put it up in the last altar as soon as you're feeling able. You sure you're all right?"

I smiled and nodded.

Then to the sun and the clouds, to Virgie and Peri and all the other Firemakers I'd met in my life without knowing it, I whispered, "I Am The Firemaker, and I am finally, permanently, all right."

CHAPTER 36

Peri's Story

I spent that night at Peri's and the next morning we went out to the garden and installed the last tile. It looked as if no other tile could ever have belonged there.

A little later, she drove me home with Dolly in her trunk. Amazingly, she had only had a few scrapes and wasn't going to need any work. After another day of resting at home I felt energized and called Peri to tell her I was coming over.

"You don't want me to come pick you up? I'd be happy to."

Thanks, but no. I actually feel wonderful and I want to ride over."

"Okay, honey, but you be real careful."

"You can count on that. I'll see you in a few minutes."

When I arrived and knocked, Peri opened the door, and after the cats and birds noisily rearranged themselves here and there as usual, she reached into her shirt pocket and handed me a card.

"Here," she said, smiling. "I forgot to give these to you. They're from those nice young paramedics I met when I was in the hospital yesterday. One of them said to give a call when you're feeling better, if you have a mind to. And I imagine you have a mind to, right?"

I smiled and nodded. "Yeah, I think I have a mind to, lump on the head and all."

Peri fixed some tea and we sat silently in the living room for perhaps ten minutes, then I asked, "Is that how it was for you, Peri? Behind the Doors, I mean?"

She chuckled. "You mean does *every* Firemaker get started on the journey through the Land Behind the Doors getting knocked unconscious off a yellow bicycle?"

I rubbed the bump on my head and laughed, "No. I mean, how did you get to the Land Behind the Doors? How did you become a Firemaker?"

Her face became thoughtful and I could see she was remembering an old and beloved story. "Oh, it was nothing like the way you entered. There are a million ways the journey can start. I did it through meditation and guided visualization, even though I'd never meditated for one second when I started. And I certainly had never been aware of being guided toward anything by anyone."

"As I told you, after Ali died and all my affairs were settled, I arranged for someone to look after the animals, locked up the garden, and went abroad to find my way again."

"Our mortgage insurance paid off the house. I knew if I was careful and invested conservatively, Ali's life insurance would be enough for me to do whatever I wanted. So off I went."

"I spent some time in Europe, then made my way on over into Africa and the Middle East with no idea where I was going, or even why, really."

"Eventually, I answered an ad placed by a university professor in Cairo and ended up working on some archaeological digs in the Valley of the Kings in Egypt for a while. It was slow, methodical work, not unlike gardening, so it was perfect for me."

"And, fortunately, the tasks I was hired to do didn't require any knowledge of archaeology, just attention to detail and patience. By then, I sure had plenty of all that."

"Anyway, after the last dig was over, I decided to see more of Egypt. That's where I met a woman on a rickety old steamboat going up the Nile."

"The encounter was similar in many ways to the day you came to me. I was just going anywhere that was away from the sadness of my recent past. But that was good enough to put me where I needed to be. We both know now that it was The City of Joy I was after."

"This woman was just waiting for me when I got on; that's all I can say. Twenty seconds after I walked on board she grabbed me by the arm and took charge. Don't misunderstand. She did it quite pleasantly. But it wasn't like I had any more choice about it than you did when Virgie sent you to me."

I smiled at the memory of the rain, my soggy hair, the collapsed paper bag and being rescued by dear Virgie. It seemed as if I'd eaten that banana light years ago, as if it was something that had happened to someone else in a distant galaxy.

Peri continued, "So, on and off for three days, she helped me attain a kind of trance state, sometimes in her stateroom, sometimes on deck under the stars in the wee hours of the morning when no other passengers were around."

"I went through seven doors, the same as you. But the *nature* of the seven doors I encountered was slightly different. While the essence of the lessons was exactly the same, they were geared to me specifically and to my level of understanding."

"I don't know what you saw, and it would be difficult to tell you what I saw. Remember this when your first novice finds you, as you found me. Her doors are not your doors or my doors. And even if you and she, or you and I, had both passed through the same door at the same time, the *way* the lessons were presented to us would still be different."

"Yes, I understand. Somehow I knew that."

Peri smiled, patted my hand, and rubbed me on the back as we stepped though her front door. "Of course you did, Helen. You're a Firemaker now."

We sat in silent companionship sipping our tea for nearly an hour as we'd done so many times before. Time was nothing to us, and her old house and the garden were the whole world right then.

When we finished, we walked our china to the kitchen. Peri took my cup and saucer and said, "Here, honey, let me take care of those. You go on home now. You don't want to overdo it. We'll pick up in the garden in the morning. Sure I can't give you a lift?"

I hugged her and said, "No, thank you, Peri. The ride over was good for me, but starting on the garden tomorrow sounds right.

I still have a lot to absorb, and I'm ready for a hot shower and a nap. But there are two more things I need to ask you."

"Okay, honey, shoot."

"First, was there another door on your journey? I don't need the details but I just want to know if there were *two* doors to choose from at the end. Is that something you can tell me?"

Peri nodded and said, "Uh-huh. There was another door."

"Wow, so that's universal to the journey, too. Fascinating. I wonder what was behind the door I *didn't* choose?"

Peri just smiled knowingly. "I'm pretty sure you'll find that out eventually, Helen."

I waited, hoping she'd say more, but she didn't.

"And what was your other question, dear?"

"It's about your name, Persephone. I know you prefer Peri and that your name is a mouthful and all of that, but – well, there's more to it than that isn't there?"

Peri smiled and patted my arm. "Yes, child, there is. If I remember correctly you're not familiar with the myth of Persephone?"

"I know virtually nothing about it, Peri, I'm embarrassed to say."

"Oh, there's nothing to be embarrassed about. The thing about myths is that the art is in the telling. And the myth of Persephone, like most really good stories, has more than one way of being told. But I'm a gardener, not a storyteller, so I'll do my best to give you the essence of it, at least as I know it."

"In Greek mythology, Persephone was the daughter of Zeus and Demeter. Her story begins on a lovely warm afternoon in a sweet meadow filled with flowers of every sort and fragrance."

"Persephone was very beautiful and many desired to be with her. Hades, god of the underworld, was among those who wanted her. He knew that Demeter would never consent to such a marriage for her daughter, so he plotted and waited."

"When his chance came, he seized the moment, burst forth from the underworld through a mighty chasm in the ground, and abducted Persephone as she gathered wild flowers for her mother."

"As you might imagine, Demeter was inconsolable over the disappearance of her daughter and when she learned where Persephone had been taken and by whom, she sent Hermes to the underworld to free her daughter."

Being a goddess, Demeter's dominion was over plants and grains and all of the growing things upon the earth. With her daughter gone, her great suffering caused Demeter to neglect her duties. Soon the fields and fruits, and the animals that fed on them, began to whither and die.

"When Hermes came for Persephone, Hades knew that Persephone was terribly lonely for her mother and the outside world and would never consent to stay with him on her own, so he devised a clever trap."

"When he released her to Hermes, he gave her several seeds to eat on the journey home."

"Unfortunately for Persephone, the pomegranate seeds were enchanted and once swallowed she was doomed to return to Hades and the underworld for part of the year, every year."

"This curse was to last throughout all time. So every year when the day approaches for Persephone to return to the underworld, Demeter's grief is so consuming that all growth stops on the surface of the world. That dormant period is called winter."

"But there's hope. At the end of Persephone's forced stay with Hades, she returns to her mother. As you can imagine, her joy is so tremendous it brings back the energy of new life onto the earth."

"Wow, what an extraordinary way to explain the seasons."

"Yes, it is. But it's more, too, Helen. Persephone's struggle between the world of light and the world of darkness is not unlike what you were told by the Firemaker about the dark, narrow cave."

"Virtually all human beings who exist on the Earth plane at any given time are some version of Persephone, constantly moving between periods of growth, light and joy, and periods of darkness and stasis."

"And even though we prefer the periods of light and obvious growth because they feel so wonderful, the times spent in stillness —in the darkness — are invaluable preparation times and opportunities for inner journeying."

"When we find ourselves apart from the light and then are returned to it, we see so much more clearly and appreciate everything so much more deeply. Without those periods of contrast, we may not choose to grow at all."

"We'd all just run around the meadow like newborn calves, and that would be fine for a while. That's what childhood's for. But it won't sustain and fulfill us over the long run."

"That's why my mother insisted that I be named Persephone, so that I would never forget that even the dark times are important and necessary."

"At some point we'll all reach the stage of growth that the Firemaker mentioned, the Unified Spirit. Then, the cycles of light and dark are no longer automatic and we can choose for ourselves how we'll grow and in what direction. Do you see?"

"Yes I do. Your mother was a wise woman and your name, Persephone, it's beautiful, just like you. Thank you for sharing all this with me."

We walked out onto the front porch and I stepped down and straddled Dolly, my old friend. "Thank you for everything, Peri. I can't think of anything else to say because there aren't enough words. But you know how deeply I mean it, right?"

"I know, dear. And you're welcome. Someone did it for me, and someday you'll do it for someone, too."

I smiled at that because I knew she was right. I would use what I experienced behind the Doors to help others to find the City of Joy inside them, just as I had been helped.

Peri winked at me as if she knew my thoughts, and then reached into the pocket of her jacket. She pulled out a little navy blue book with gold lettering on the cover and handed it to me. There was a bright red ribbon around it, tied in a bow.

"When you find the time and things have settled down a bit, you'll want to read this. It belongs to you now."

"Run along before it starts to rain again. And watch those brakes on the other side of that hill. Goodbye for tonight my dear little Firemaker. I'll see you here tomorrow."

I smiled and nodded, accepted the book, and slipped it into my backpack without reading the cover, somehow knowing that was the proper way to do it. "Thank you again, Peri. I'll see you tomorrow."

At home, I let the book sit in my backpack for the rest of the day and contented myself with experiencing this whole new way of being. I was happy and calm in a way I'd never, ever been. Everything was in alignment and I was whole.

Before my journey, I'd thought of my future as something created entirely out of the past. If you'd asked me how I viewed it, I'd have said it looked like a long, dark road of mind-numbing work and perpetually delayed fulfillment.

But life looked different now; it looked flexible and forgiving. There was time to grow and loads of resources built right inside of me to help me get to where I wanted to be.

The fulfillment of my Downstream Dream was coming closer to me as I was moving with Life's flow toward it. Believing that, knowing I was becoming what I sought to be, what I held outside myself as worthy and whole inside, gave me a feeling of release.

If I kept moving forward, following my inner compass, I would live out the wonderful Possible Futures I glimpsed in the Pool. The visions I had seen there were as clear and bright to me as the debris in the Swamp of the Past had been murky and dark.

Living each day as merely another step in an interminable forced march that began with my birth had doomed me to years of regret, loneliness, and fear. I'd had enough of that.

The movement of life is *toward* us, not away. The beginning and the ending exist on a continuum that can only be fully understood from a larger perspective. Now that I had that, everything was changed.

Life seems as opposite from what I once believed about the way it worked as anything could be. Yet nothing outside me was different. The world still spins on its axis and orbits the sun. Earth is still a beautiful blue sphere revolving in a sea vast beyond measure.

Only I am different. *I am different!* I belong in the world, and I am not alone. The Universe has a place for me. It isn't for me to figure it all out; it's for me to open myself to what lies ahead, to listen to and bring forth what lives within. It's for me to make new fires that bring light and warmth and safety into the world from the sparks of my little piece of the sun.

This is what I was born to do.

CHAPTER 37

The Little Blue Book

After dinner that night, I pulled out the little blue book Peri had given me and untied the red ribbon. The cover was made of cloth and the title written in fancy gold script. I opened it and read:

The Legacy of The Firemaker

Throughout all of human history there have been a rare and precious few called Firemaker.

It is they who bring the new into the old and help expand human potential in the world.

It is they who accomplish great things and lead humanity toward soaring new vistas filled with astounding Possible Futures.

They lead the world out of seemingly impossible dilemmas that, if left to unfold unchecked, would dash all hope and snuff out the warming fires of joy and compassion forever.

The names of those Firemakers are known to many.

But there are also Firemakers who are ordinary in appearance and work quietly and without fanfare, doing extraordinary things that are vital to human survival.

Their deeds often go unnoticed and unheralded, and their names unrecorded in the books of history.

It matters not whether individual Firemakers are visible or unnoticed, or how their work is done.

They are nonetheless the creators of the Flame of Truth and agents of growth and change for the betterment for all. And what of the rest of humanity?

The work of the many is born out of the ideas, discoveries and efforts of Firemakers—all of it.

Once a Firemaker ignites the Flame of Truth, others associate themselves with the new light and heat, using those elements to produce valuable and needed things.

These people are The Flamekeepers.

Most are Flamekeepers. They do not invent new ideas or discover new cures. They apply the knowledge brought into the world by the Firemakers.

The differences between Firemakers and Flamekeepers are not as dramatic as they might seem.

Everyone has the potential to become a Firemaker, to carry that inner spark from place to place in their lives, lighting up the world wherever they go, whatever they do.

Most secretly feel that potential, that special thing waiting just beyond their present understanding. They long for this something they cannot name, often mistakenly looking outside at the world instead of inside themselves.

Most will never do the searching and work necessary to discover and use the Inner Flame. And so the world is filled with people standing next to the warming fires created by a very special few.

This is neither bad nor good. At this stage of human evolution, it is simply the way of things.

The general belief of humankind is that people must stay in place, tethered to whatever fire they are beside at birth. It could be the fire of the birth family, town, country or traditions in which they were raised.

This is the choice of most people: To avoid the pain of uncertainty and turn away from the risk of adventure, never daring to imagine that they could travel elsewhere and make their own fire whenever necessary.

Thus, this is the fate of most human beings, and while it seems as if set in stone by outside forces or immutable societal laws, in truth it is often self-imposed.

A Firemaker is a person with a piece of the sun that never goes out. From its warmth and light a Firemaker makes magical sparks that build and renew what is nascent or outworn.

A Firemaker can generate the Fire of Truth anywhere, under any conditions, and then step back and allow others to choose for themselves if they will embrace it.

A Firemaker does not judge others or their actions, but simply brings forth fire, warmth and light and lets others choose to use it or not.

And you may ask, "With the Firemakers here to show truth and create good, why is there so much madness and sorrow in the world?"

The answer is twofold: First, nothing but Cosmic Order usurps personal will, even when it is used for destruction and chaos. And Cosmic Order includes allowing personal will in many situations, much of the time.

Second, all illness comes from a broken heart.

To intentionally do harm is an act that spins out from an illness of the mind. And that illness only exists because the heart of that person, or someone close to that person, has been broken. No matter how evil the doer may seem, at the center is a broken heart.

That reality, expanded to extremes, creates the third group of powerful and destructive human beings, those who will not do the work of creating or tending the Fire of Truth, yet crave the power of fire all the same.

These people are called Shadowmakers.

The way of the Shadowmakers is to dash out of the darkness, steal a small burning branch from a fire created by others and then run away with it into the night.

The horrible despots of history are Shadowmakers, plundering enough fuel to ignite raging wildfires of destruction across much of the world.

Shadowmakers create nothing that lasts. They only steal fire and then pollute its beauty, trample on its truth and damage the fragile balance of the Earth.

The least powerful in this group, the lost and the desperate, are unable to live without such things as too much strong drink, dark potions and dangerous pursuits, and eventually find no additional fuel.

As their stolen branches burn out, they are swallowed up by the darkness.

A Firemaker comes into being as a result of much slow, methodical work. This is a process of winnowing away the negative and illuminating what is good in human beings, then connecting the good to all that individuals have the potential to be.

Brave adventurer, you have been led to this moment by other Firemakers and your Greater Self and are, at last, free to pursue the Path of becoming a Unified Spirit.

You are a Firemaker now, and whenever you need guidance or strength, simply say these words, then be still and wait for the answers you seek, for they will come.

Say...

I AM THE FIREMAKER

And it is so.

Ω

About the Author

Marina Walker Rose, PhD

If you arrive early enough (tuck your shoes by the door when you come in), you just might find Marina Walker Rose, paintbrush in hand, in the sparkling cool of the morning, communing with the *spirits of color* and the loamy new green of growing things. Working from the happy chaos of her seaside creation center, Little Bridge Studios, Marina Rose joyfully wields words and paint, unabashedly inspiring fellow Cosmic Explorers on their journey of remembering *who they are.*

Author, internationally recognized abstract artist, visionary psychotherapist, and mystic storyteller, she weaves a wide new world of inner magic and healing freedom in her novel *Seven Doors of The Firemaker: A Personal and Planetary Adventure*, and illustrated *The Firemaker Companion Notebook: A Very Human Cosmic Explorer's Guide.*

To learn more about Marina Walker Rose, her books and paintings, and for information about special Seven Doors events and other adventures, visit MarinaWalkerRose.com.

Thank you for reading the Seven Doors of the Firemaker!

If you would like to apply the concepts that Helen learned in your life, you are invited to get the companion notebook, also by Marina Walker Rose. *The Firemarker Companion Notebook: A Very Human Cosmic Explorer's Guide* is full of beautiful full-color original art, journaling opportunities, and information that will aid you in discovering more about yourself. Based on the concepts in the novel and Marina's years as a therapist, the companion notebook will take you on a gentle journey to discovering your own Downstream Dream.

You can learn more about the notebook by visiting MarinaWalkerRose.com

There's a special gift waiting for you there too at MarinaWalkerRose.com/readergift

Did you like this book?

Please help us spread the word about this book by sharing it with your friends and leaving an honest review on Amazon.com. In our digital world, book reviews are the most important way to share good books with the world.

To leave a review visit Amazon.com and put Seven Doors of the Firemaker into the search box. Then, scroll down the page a bit until you are prompted to leave a review. You can leave a review even if you purchased the book outside of Amazon.

Thank you very much!

Made in the USA
Monee, IL
28 November 2020